Sher

Boulevard Assassin

John Hall

First published in 1998 by
Breese Books
This revised edition published in 2020 by
Baker Street Studios Ltd and
The Irregular Special Press for
Breese Books
Endeavour House
170 Woodland Road, Sawston
Cambridge, CB22 3DX, UK

ISBN: 978 0 947533 52 6

Cover Illustration: The Porte Saint-Martin and the
Boulevard Saint-Denis from a postcard circa 1900.

Typeset in 8/11/20pt Palatino

This book is dedicated to
all **The Northern Musgraves**
and in particular to
the **Consultants**

One

The Banque de France occupies Number 1 and Number 3 of the Rue de La Vrillière, Paris. At Number 2 in the same road is an old house decorated with turrets and possessed of a curious spiral balcony. From his post at the main entrance to the Bank, Monsieur Auguste Vauban, the doorman, could – with the exercise of a little ingenuity – see the old house at Number 2, and he spent many hours wondering about it. He wondered who had built it, who had owned it and lived in it, and he wondered what they had thought as they had stood on that odd balcony, or climbed to the turrets for a view over Paris.

Sometimes he would fancy that the turrets were battlements indeed, that they were perhaps part of the great works constructed by his illustrious, but – alas! – unrelated, namesake. He would picture to himself the great men of old, those gallant cavaliers and lords and kings of whom he had so often read, coming galloping down the familiar street hot from some battle, and ready for a night's boasting and carousing.

And if, on occasion, Auguste imagined that there was some beautiful woman in the old house, in mortal danger from which only one bold, resourceful man could save her, well, Auguste was a Frenchman; and besides, his work was not invariably of the most exciting. Indeed, if one is to be honest, it was frequently downright dull.

There were exceptions, to be sure, to the everyday routine. Auguste's working hours were not entirely devoid of all interest, particularly when a member of the aristocracy visited the Bank, which was by no means a rare occurrence. Such visits were usually a matter of business, as one may suppose; but sometimes they were for pleasure.

The guidebooks tell us that the building which houses the Bank was formerly the Hôtel de La Vrilliére, that it was built by Mansart in 1635, and that it was at one time the residence of the Princesse de Lamballe. The Bank retains the eighteenth-century Galerie Dorée, which may be seen by interested visitors who have first applied in writing to the Governor of the Bank. The admirable Baedeker even provides a specimen letter of application, for the benefit of English *milords* and others whose knowledge of the French language begins and ends with the fact that the pen of one's aunt resides upon the table of one's gardener's uncle – interesting enough information in itself, *bien entendu*, and raising many interesting questions in the mind of the acute reasoner besides; but then perhaps not of any great use in the more mundane business of *la vie quotidienne*.

On the morning of St Valentine's Day, 1891, Auguste Vaudan was in his usual place. It was a Saturday, and Auguste naturally looked forward with some degree of pleasurable anticipation to the following day, when he intended to make a little excursion with his family. The Bank was busy enough, but there was nothing out of the ordinary, nothing to prevent Auguste's mind wandering to the little inn which he knew well, an inn on the outskirts of the city, an inn where the red wine was as rough as the landlord's invective, but where the fish was a feast for the gods. Auguste thought of the wine, and the fish, and of the countryside, which would just be starting to rally after the horrid drabness of winter.

Auguste's reverie was suddenly interrupted by the arrival of a carriage. Auguste immediately took a couple of steps forward, for there was money here. The carriage itself, the pair of greys which pulled it, and the coat of arms on the door, all these things conspired together to make Auguste's back just a little straighter, and his salute just a little crisper, than would normally have been the case. The man who descended from the carriage was just what Auguste would have expected. The aristocratic profile, the heavy diamond ring, the huge pearl in the cravat, the military bearing; these alone would have been sufficient recommendation, without the large, stiff, embossed card, or the *laissez-passer* signed by the Governor, which the visitor rather shyly proffered to Auguste – to Auguste, for all the world as if he were the manager himself ! And if the name on the card meant nothing to Auguste, then at least he knew that it would assuredly mean a great deal to his opposite number at the door of the Bank of England! One could see that at a glance!

Accordingly, Auguste lost no time in summoning one of the senior clerks to conduct this English *milord* to the office of the assistant manager charged with entertaining such visitors. Auguste was rewarded with a smile which – almost – compensated for the meagre tip, itself a final and incontrovertible proof that the visitor was an English aristocrat.

In the office of the assistant manager, despite the favourable nature of the Englishman's outward appearance, the visitor's card, passport, and the letter from the Governor were all scrutinized with greater care than Auguste had bestowed upon them. Everything quickly proved to be in order, and the visitor was conducted to the Galerie Dorée, where his delighted reaction and murmurs of appreciation showed him to be a man of the utmost discernment. The assistant manager did not, of course, leave even so distinguished a foreigner alone, but waited discreetly on one side whilst the visitor saw all that there was to see, and made some notes with a gold pencil in a leather-bound book.

At the conclusion of the visit, the stranger asked if the assistant manager would care to improve their acquaintance over luncheon. The assistant manager felt that politeness required that he should show some hesitation; but when the stranger mentioned the restaurant which he proposed to visit, then hesitation turned at once to acquiescence. Auguste, still at his post, saw the stranger leave in the company of the assistant manager. Auguste gave the stranger his best salute; the stranger greeted Auguste almost as an old friend, and handed him a tip which more than compensated for his previous rather parsimonious behaviour.

The luncheon was everything the assistant manager had expected and more, although the conversation was somewhat limited. Indeed, there was really but one topic – the stranger asked certain very searching questions about the running of the Bank, the various safeguards and precautions against theft, and the like. The assistant manager was naturally flattered that the stranger was so interested, and was more than pleased to answer fully and frankly all that was asked.

At a somewhat later hour than usual, the assistant manager returned, alone, to the Bank. He greeted Auguste with considerably more warmth than was his wont, and Auguste, his mind filled with thoughts alike of expensive luncheons and the money seated snugly in his trousers pocket, gave a conspiratorial grin. The assistant manager then returned to his own office, there to doze unobserved.

Auguste, meantime, turned his thoughts to the money which was burning a hole in his pocket. He pictured to himself the large, chocolate-brown notes; he counted them over and over in his mind; and above all he saw the Sunday luncheon which the money would buy, a luncheon that should not disgrace the assistant manager of the Banque de France – nay, that would not bring a frown to the brow of Monsieur le Gouverneur himself!

Auguste's delightful reverie was – for the second time that day – rudely interrupted after some thirty minutes by the arrival of two carriages, driven hard and with obvious urgency. The occupants leapt down almost before the carriages had properly come to a halt, and came up the steps to where the astonished Auguste stood.

The man at the head of the little group, a tall, thin man of striking appearance, fairly raced ahead of the others. He stopped in his headlong flight before Auguste and rapped out in a staccato fashion, 'You have had a visitor today, is that not so? A man of such-and-such a description, who wished to visit the Galerie Dorée?'

'It is so, Monsieur,' stammered Auguste.

'Is he still here?'

Auguste, his head whirling, could only stare at the man. The second of the group, a shorter, stout man who had taken the steps rather more sedately, had arrived by this time, and said, 'Come, my good man. This is police business,' and he held up a card which identified him as being from the office of the prefect of police. 'Is this man still in the building?' he asked.

'No, Monsieur. He saw the assistant manager ... they had luncheon together ...'

'And where is the assistant manager?' asked the tall man.

Auguste stammered out some directions, and the tall man raced off through the building.

The stout man looked sternly at Auguste. 'You are to remain here,' said he, 'and keep a close watch on all who enter or leave. In particular, you are to watch for the man who was here this morning ... for I can tell you frankly that he was an imposter, a villain of the deepest dye. Should you see him enter, you are to send a message at once to myself, or to Mr Sherlock Holmes.' And he nodded after the tall man, who was now out of sight. 'You are not to leave your post until we shall tell you that all is in order. You understand?'

Auguste nodded dumbly, and the stout man followed Sherlock Holmes into the Bank. The last two members of the group, a tall, thin man dressed in black, and a second rather stout gentleman whom Auguste recognized at once as a director of the Bank, looked gravely at Auguste, shook their heads sadly in unison, and followed their colleagues.

Auguste stood in the doorway, not knowing what to think. He looked at the driver of the nearest carriage, a question in his eyes, but the driver merely shrugged, as one who should say, 'There is no use asking me, *mon ami*, for who can say what the great men may do next?'

But still – Sherlock Holmes! The fact that the prefecture of police was involved was exciting enough, provoking enough – perhaps bad enough – of course, but that the famous Sherlock

Holmes should himself take a hand! Auguste knew of Monsieur Holmes, of course – who did not? – for all the world knew that the man was no mere English *milord*, but a true Frenchman himself, though obliged – alas! – to hide his identity in perfidious Albion, doubtless for reasons political or amorous, one had no doubt. Perhaps both; with such a man, who could say? *Merde*, thought Auguste – his invariable first reaction to any crisis – and then, as his head cleared slightly, *Mais qu'est-ce qui est arrivé?*

Similar thoughts were going through the head of the assistant manager, as he stared, unbelieving, at Sherlock Holmes and his companions. If it were not for the presence of the director, who was of course well known to the assistant manager by sight, then the assistant manager would never have taken seriously the fantastic allegation that had just been put to him – no, not even though it had been the famous Monsieur Sherlock Holmes and the representative of the prefect of police who had made it! 'But – but everything was in order, I assure you!' was all he could eventually stammer out.

'A clever forgery,' said Holmes incisively. 'Do you know who that was?'

'But of course! His card, his passport ...'

'Forged!' cried Holmes. 'That was Arsène Jupin himself!'

The assistant manager, overcome, sat down and mopped his brow. Jupin! Arsène Jupin! The notorious jewel thief! Jupin! As famous as Sherlock Holmes himself – more famous than Holmes, in France at any rate! Jupin, whose exploits were known to every reader of *Le Miroir*, the newspaper which, so rumour had it, Jupin himself owned!

Holmes went on, 'I am only thankful that we arrived before any real damage was done.'

The representative of the prefect cleared his throat with evident hesitation. 'I take it we are all satisfied that no damage *was* done, then?'

The assistant manager mopped his brow. 'Nothing, Monsieur! ... I assure you ... nothing has been taken from the Bank! It is impossible!'

'But you say that he was asking questions throughout your meal?' asked Holmes.

'Indeed, Monsieur. He asked about the guards, the vaults ...'

'The vaults?' snapped Holmes.

'The vaults, Monsieur. They contain not merely notes but gold, both bullion and specie, together with a not inconsiderable quantity of diamonds ...'

'You were not so foolish as to let him roam round these famous vaults, though?' asked the man from the prefect's office, sceptically.

'Indeed not, Monsieur! But I may ... that is ... he was naturally interested ... and yet I swear I told him nothing ... nothing that is not common knowledge!'

'Rumour has it,' said Holmes, 'that these same vaults may be flooded with water, or with some mephitic vapour, by the mere turning of a tap?'

The assistant manager, now very conscious of the fact that the manager – who should by rights, of course, have dealt with this sort of disturbing occurrence – had left early, it being a Saturday, looked anxiously at the director, who nodded discreetly to indicate that he should answer.

'They are merely rumours, Monsieur,' said the assistant manager. 'Rumours which we do not take the trouble to counter, since they may well discourage those criminals who persist in taking them seriously. The vaults are, however, supplied with a quantity of sand, stored in bags which can be piled upon the valuables in case of need.'

'Sand?' asked Holmes.

'Sand, Monsieur,' said the director. 'To prevent fire from reaching the notes, let us say; or to prevent damage by artillery bombardment, such as we Parisians have unfortunately experienced even in my own lifetime.'

Holmes nodded. 'I comprehend. The sand may perhaps be of some use?' He waved a hand to indicate the tall, thin man, who had thus far taken no part in the conversation. 'This gentleman,' he told the assistant manager, 'is from the office of

11

the public auditor. What,' he asked the auditor, 'is your opinion, Monsieur?'

The auditor looked from one to another of his audience with a curious oscillating motion of his head. 'The gold is, of course, hard to move, due to its great weight,' said he. 'And we might place the sand-bags upon the notes, to make it difficult to shift them. There was, however, mention of diamonds, I think?' and he stared at the assistant manager with a piercing gaze.

'Indeed, Monsieur! A vast quantity, and of the most valuable.'

'That is indeed a danger,' said the auditor. 'Diamonds, you understand, being light and, as it were, portable ...'

'I understand!' cried the assistant manager. 'Why, a determined rogue with large pockets might carry upon his person a fortune worth a king's ransom!'

Holmes rubbed his chin thoughtfully. There was a moment's silence, then he laughed aloud. 'And four determined men?' he asked the assistant manager.

'Monsieur?'

'Well, are there more diamonds than the four of us ...' and he waved a hand to indicate his companions – 'might transport in our two carriages?'

'No, Monsieur, not many more. But ... but I fear I hardly comprehend you ...'

'We shall have this rogue Jupin by the heels!' said Holmes with a chuckle. 'Do you, Monsieur, set your fellows to work piling the sand-bags upon the notes to make them immovable ... and upon the gold, too, should you see fit. And set a guard upon the vaults when once that is done. Meantime, I and these other gentlemen will take the diamonds away with us for safe-keeping.'

'Take the diamonds!' cried the assistant manager. 'But ... but where to?'

Holmes laughed. 'Why, to the prefecture of police!' said he. 'Let the villain try to take them from there! Monsieur the Director here will, naturally, come along with us, as a representative of the Bank, and to oversee the whole affair.'

The assistant manager looked at the director, hoping for guidance. 'Monsieur?'

The director thought for a moment, then nodded agreement. 'It is the safest way. There will be no risk, so long as I accompany the stones.'

The assistant manager, pleased that the decision was not his, reached into his waistcoat pocket for the key to the vault. He was about to speak when without any warning the door flew open, and one of the senior clerks burst in unceremoniously and cried, 'Monsieur! A thousand pardons, but there is some trouble at the main door!'

'Trouble?' asked Holmes at once.

'The doorman, Vauban ... he is fighting with a man! Vauban keeps saying he is "an imposter", Monsieur! Vauban is asking for Monsieur the Director, for Monsieur the Assistant Manager ... but above all he asks for Monsieur Sherlock Holmes!'

The assistant manager replaced the key in his waistcoat pocket, and moved quickly behind his desk. In all that illustrious company, he alone seemed able to speak. 'An imposter!' he cried. 'What, another! But wait ... I see! This must be the man who called here this morning! It is Jupin, then! Messieurs, we have him already!'

'It is not the man who called this morning, Monsieur,' said the clerk, recovering his poise somewhat.

'What?'

'Not at all, Monsieur! Did I myself not bring this morning's visitor to see Monsieur the Assistant Manager? I should know him again, anywhere! This is another man. But the strange thing is ...'

'Yes?'

'He himself claims to be Monsieur Sherlock Holmes! He must be a madman! Unless indeed it is Vauban who has gone mad!' said the clerk.

Holmes, who had been showing every sign of agitation during this exchange, spoke at last. 'This is not a madman, Monsieur,' said he, 'but a clever distraction! Do you not see?' he appealed to the others. 'Whilst this villain is creating a disturbance at the front door, impersonating me, Jupin and the

13

rest of his fellows are already entering the Bank by the back! We must go there at once! This way, is it not?' And before anyone could stop him, he raced off down the corridor. The man from the prefect's office looked at the man from the auditor's office, then, without a word being said, both men turned and ran off after Holmes.

The astonished clerk looked from the director to the assistant manager. 'Messieurs? What shall I do?'

'Call the police!' said the assistant manager decisively.

The clerk nodded, turned and ran off.

'But what is happening?' the director managed at last.

'Monsieur, I do not know. All I know is that the key to the vault is still here, upon my watch-chain …' and the assistant manager produced the key from his waistcoat pocket, and held it up, before replacing it – 'and there it stays! I shall not give it up for you, begging your pardon, Monsieur; nor for the entire Board of Directors; nor for the Governor himself … no, nor for the very Prince of Darkness and all his fallen angels, though they drag me down to the Pit!'

The director stared at the assistant manager for a long moment, then took hold of his shoulders. The assistant manager, suspecting further villainy, made to step back, but the director merely kissed him on both cheeks before remarking, 'Were it in my gift, Monsieur, you should have the Legion of Honour!'

Meantime, heroic deeds were being done at the main entrance to the Bank. It may perhaps be that Auguste Vauban has hitherto appeared in this narrative as somewhat effete, a dreamer, a man concerned only with thoughts of Sunday lunch with his family. Nothing could be farther from the truth: Auguste was a stout fellow in every sense. He was the scion of a long line of farmers, and if he was not exactly quick of wit, then at least he was strong of arm.

For all that, thought Auguste, it was the devil's own job to subdue this villain, this imposter, this man who had the audacity to pretend to be Sherlock Holmes! But, with the aid of a couple of his fellow guards, and some of the more daring of the clerks, Auguste managed to keep the rascal quiet enough, until the arrival of Monsieur Dubuque of the Paris police, who – as an old customer of the Bank – was well enough known to Auguste by sight.

Dubuque had also known Mr Sherlock Holmes for some years, and – when once Auguste had been persuaded to allow the 'villain' to stand up – Dubuque unhesitatingly identified the supposed imposter as the real, the only, Sherlock Holmes.

Auguste was apologetic, but what else could he have done, in all conscience? Sherlock Holmes spoke quietly to himself, in an abstracted fashion, for some considerable time; Auguste did not understand the words, but he could follow the general sense, and it rather spoiled the rest of his day, and cast a blight over his Sunday luncheon party to boot.

Naturally, by the time the truth had emerged, it was too late to pursue the fake Holmes, or the equally spurious representative of the prefect of police; and above all it was too late to follow the unassuming-looking 'auditor', who was, as the real Holmes told Dubuque bitterly, none other than the infamous Professor Ja.

Two

Mr Sherlock Holmes leaned back in his chair, and looked across at me. 'Well, Watson?'

'All imposters?' said I, incredulous. 'The whole lot of them? All members of the same gang ... the Moriarty gang?'

Holmes nodded. 'The first rogue impersonated an English gentleman; then the others made a point of seeming to reveal that it was an imposture, and that the visitor was really Jupin, whilst themselves actually impersonating the forces of law and order!'

'Including you?'

Holmes laughed. 'As you say. Damnable impudence!' He grew more serious. 'It was a master stroke to say that it was Jupin, of course.'

'Indeed,' said I, 'for he is as famous in France as ...'

'My blushes, Watson!'

'I was about to say, "... as he is unknown in England"!'

Holmes laughed.

I went on, 'I suppose that it was *not* Jupin, though? After all, it is exactly the sort of daring thing he would do!'

Holmes – who had been involved once or twice with Jupin in the past, at the request of the French police – considered this a moment before shaking his head. 'You mean that Jupin himself might genuinely have had designs on the Bank of France? It would be a monstrous coincidence indeed!' said he, adding with a smile, 'Even you would hardly dare employ it in your accounts!'

17

'I would not be too sure, Holmes! But I agree, it would be stretching credibility somewhat if one set of villains had used the designs of another set! But I meant rather ... might Jupin not have been a member of the gang?'

Holmes reflected. 'I think not. He prefers to work alone; and besides, although he is criminal, he is a gentleman, he has his own standards, his own code. And one cannot truthfully say that of Moriarty or any of his associates. No, Jupin was not involved, save for the use of his name.'

'The gang used one of their own men, then, to impersonate Jupin, who was then to impersonate an English aristocrat?'

'Delicious, is it not?'

'And the rest were all similarly imposters?' I shook my head in disbelief.

'Imposters, to a man. But clever imposters, all. All, that is, save the director of the Bank. He was genuine enough ... the others had fooled him completely, made him think that there was a very real and pressing danger to the Bank's deposits, in order that he might go with them to the Bank ... where, of course, he was known to be genuine ... and so lend verisimilitude to their story. And then, naturally, when he learned that some mysterious "stranger" had called that very morning ... and that the visitor was Jupin! ... well, that served to confirm the whole tale, and any lingering doubts he may have entertained vanished at once. Needless to say, the unfortunate director was the only one whom the police managed to arrest!' He grew more serious. 'And at that he was lucky, Watson, for there is no doubt whatsoever in my mind that Moriarty and the others would have killed him out of hand when once they were fairly away from the Bank with the diamonds.'

'It was a daring plan.'

'Such merit as it had lay in its daring, and its simplicity,' said Holmes thoughtfully. 'After all, what could be simpler than to walk into a bank and ask the assistant manager to let you roam around the vaults and walk out with your pockets stuffed with diamonds?'

'It was risky, though?'

'Perhaps not as risky as might at first appear,' said Holmes. 'Their *bona fides* seemed impeccable ... there was a genuine director, who was known to the clerks and the managers; there was an elderly, and clearly respectable auditor; there was a representative from the prefecture of police; and, of course, lastly ...'

'But by no means least ...'

Holmes laughed. 'It was unfortunate for them that I had pursued Moriarty to Paris,' said he. 'They could not have taken that into account, although perhaps they ought to have done so.'

'Moriarty, at any rate, took a great risk, by appearing in person, so to speak.'

'You must realize,' said Holmes, 'that his intention was to move his field of operations into France, and thence ... I have no doubt at all ... to the rest of Europe, like some monstrous plague. And, like any other businessman, he naturally needed capital, funds for this expansion. He had already made one attempt upon the deposits of the Banque de France ... although that attempt took place in London ... and he simply tried again, but this time he did not leave it up to a subordinate.'

'Whatever one may think of him, he was not lacking in courage or ingenuity. It was a daring and outrageous exploit. And it is undoubtedly an interesting story,' I said. 'Yes, much might be made of it, with a little imagination.'

'Imagination?' said Holmes with some annoyance. 'And are the mere facts not sufficient in themselves? Must they be dressed up with French phrases dimly remembered from one's distant schooldays and hurriedly ... though all too often inadequately ... checked with an elementary grammar before dispatch to the publisher? Must the account consist of adjectives following, rather than preceding, their nouns, and peppered withal with exclamation marks, in order to give a ... a ... what can I call it ... an authentic Parisian atmosphere?'

I surreptitiously jotted a note on my cuff – "lots excl mks!!!" – before bothering to reply to this calumny. 'Modern readers are by no means the unsophisticated creatures they once were, Holmes,' said I. 'The Board Schools have made epicures of them. They demand a certain amount of background, of descriptive material. "The human angle", as our American friends would term it.'

'Oh, well! If you are really going ...'

'I could, perhaps, write it largely from the point of view of one of the relatively minor characters, the assistant manager, or the doorman, say. Yes, that would be one way.'

Three years of travel studying the fatalistic philosophies of the mysterious East had evidently done nothing to sweeten Holmes's temper. 'The doorman? And what the devil had the doorman to do with anything, pray? Beyond sitting on my head and thereby preventing me laying my hands upon the rogues, that is?'

'Human interest, Holmes.'

'But how can you tell his story? Why, you do not even know the fellow's name!'

'No more does anyone else, Holmes! Who can say that it is not what I choose it to be? And there are plenty of biographical encyclopaedias!'

Holmes emitted a sound which I can only politely describe as a snort of derision, and lit his briar, which had gone out whilst he was telling me the tale which I have just set down for you – in a slightly modified form, for it cannot be denied that Holmes's own version was somewhat lacking in that human interest which he sometimes so disparaged.

'Not that your account was in any sense uninteresting of itself, of course,' I hastened to add, trying my best to mollify him. 'Indeed, it is of the first importance to anyone who ... like myself ... would wish to understand your pursuit of Professor Moriarty.'

Holmes, almost his old self again, nodded. 'It was a long and very involved pursuit,' he said. 'The episode I have just recounted was by no means the most daring of Moriarty's exploits, nor the most difficult of my investigations.'

'Do you say so? The others must have been interesting indeed! And Moriarty managed to escape so often! The world is fortunate that you were finally able to pursue your investigations to such good effect.[1] Just think how different things might have been had Moriarty survived the Falls of the Reichenbach!'

'Indeed,' murmured Holmes. And he added hastily, almost as if to change the subject, 'How is the sale of your practice coming along?'

It was towards the end of June, 1894. Holmes had been back in London for almost three months, and he had prevailed upon me to sell my little practice in Kensington and move back to my old lodgings in 221B Baker Street. For some reason which I could not begin to explain, although I had known so much sadness there the practice still had some sentimental attraction for me, and I had accordingly set upon it a higher figure than I thought it warranted, half hoping that the elevated price would discourage prospective buyers; but a young Dr Verner had paid what I asked at once, almost without properly looking the place over. It was not until later that I learned that he was a distant relative of Holmes's, and that Holmes had advanced the money for the purchase.

To a certain extent, Holmes and I were having to get to know each other all over again. His three years in the wilds had had their effect; and I dare say that my own happy marriage and sad bereavement had gone some way to changing me, too. But yet we had settled down happily enough a decade before, and we were not all that different now, save for being a little older and perhaps – one can dream – even a little wiser, so that I had hopes that things would quickly be back as they had once been.

The one thing I really dreaded was boredom, for I knew that inactivity would cause Holmes to relapse into those habits which I had so often, and for so long, had reason to condemn. Inactivity, boredom, those were the demons I feared most where Holmes was concerned. His capture of Colonel Sebastian Moran, which I have recorded under the title of *The Empty House*, was the one and only approach to a case which Holmes had undertaken since his return to London, and even then it was Inspector Lestrade who had – at Holmes's own

---

[1] See *The Travels of Sherlock Holmes*.

express request – received the credit for Moran's arrest. The public, that 'great unobservant public', as Holmes had once called it, remained in ignorance of the very fact that Holmes was still alive, and we had few callers in that summer of '94. It was to keep Holmes from the horrors of the hypodermic syringe and the cocaine bottle that I had prompted him to recount something of that long, lonely and difficult investigation into the Moriarty gang which had occupied the winter of 1890 and '91.

Before I could reply, Holmes leaned forward, then suddenly straightened up. I could swear that he sniffed the very air, like an old hound on the scent. 'You hear that, Watson?'

I listened. 'Street noises, Holmes? A cab rattling along. Several cabs. An argument going on. The newspaper vendor, crying his wares. That's all I hear.'

'Ah, Watson, Watson! You hear, but you do not observe! The newspaper vendor, my boy! Listen! You hear his intonation? It is almost exultation!'

'Doggerel, Holmes, doggerel. A sad misuse of the English …'

'Doggerel be damned! There's murder in that cry, Watson! Murder, mutilation, and mayhem!' He leapt to his feet and rang the bell vigorously, then, with a curious echo of the very metaphor that had occurred to me, he added, 'The old hound may have found a new line to follow yet! Now, Billy,' he told the page boy who appeared in answer to the bell, 'I require a copy of every newspaper you can find … and quickly, mind!'

'Yessir!' The page ran out of the room.

'We may have a case, Watson! A case, at long last!'

'Part of me could wish it were so,' said I. 'But yet it will be at the cost of some poor devil's life or happiness.'

'H'mm.' Holmes was subdued for a moment only, then he said, 'Ah, but the damage is already done. Were you to be called out to attend some medical emergency, you would hardly hold yourself to blame for its occurrence, now would you? You would merely set about doing what you could to amend matters.'

'Perhaps you are right. Ah, here is Billy.'

'Put them down anywhere, Billy,' said Holmes eagerly. He seized the nearest newspaper. 'Good Lord!'

I picked up another newspaper, glanced at the bold headline – 'PRESIDENT OF FRANCE ASSASSINATED' – and echoed his sentiment. 'Great heavens, Holmes!' I read on, to learn that President Sadi Carnot had been stabbed whilst in Lyons; the assailant being one of those misguided zealots who call themselves 'anarchists'.

Holmes had flung himself into a chair, and read in silence for a time. Then he threw the newspaper down, and picked up another. 'A bad business, this, Watson. What have you there?'

'I fancy the accounts are all broadly similar,' said I. 'It says here that the assassin was taken by an angry crowd, which is something at any rate.'

'And what use ...' Holmes broke off, picked up another newspaper, and another. 'They all have the same tale, as you say.' He subsided in his chair. 'A bad business indeed, Watson. Pass me the matches, and prepare to listen whilst I tell you my thoughts on this matter.'

I threw my tobacco pouch across to him. 'I shall be most interested,' said I.

'You must first cast your mind back to the winter of 1890,' said Holmes. 'I had become aware ... no matter exactly how ... of the fact that Professor Moriarty was extending his operations to the Continent, to France, in fact. I followed him there ...'

'And that is how you came to frustrate his designs on the diamonds held by the Bank of France?'

Holmes nodded. 'You will recall that when I called upon you in the April of 1891, I mentioned that Professor Moriarty had given me a list of the occasions upon which I had incommoded him?'

'I fancy that I noted the fact in my account of what I called *The Final Problem.*'

'I fancy that you did. Along with much else that was sensational, if not downright inaccurate. Be all that as it may, Moriarty was in the process of opening a branch office, so to speak, in France, and he had a trusty lieutenant, the direct equivalent in the French gang of Colonel Sebastian Moran in the English gang.'

'And the name of this French lieutenant?' I asked.

Holmes frowned. 'That is one thing that I did not manage to find out. I imagine he has a dozen aliases. Certainly, he is a master of disguise and an accomplished actor, for it was he who had the deuced nerve to impersonate me in that Bank of France affair! And the doorman of the Bank ... the prospective hero of your sensational narrative, my dear Watson, and the man who prevented the immediate arrest of Moriarty ... this doorman swore that he was the very image of me!'

'Well, it seems to me that the resemblance is significant,' said I. 'At least we know that he resembles you in a general sense, height, weight, and what have you, be his face raddled never so heavily.'

'Watson, Watson! Have I myself not demonstrated to you on more than one occasion that a man may take a foot off his height without so very much trouble? It is inconvenient, to be sure, even painful; but it can be done. And to add a few inches is less trouble still, for a thick-soled boot, a top hat, will do much to fool the casual observer.'

'But his weight? His build?'

'I will allow you that.'

I sat up. 'You may have to allow me more, Holmes. Does it not seem to you that Moriarty may perhaps have chosen his representative simply because of the resemblance to you? That the professor had planned to use him as a decoy in some villainy of the very sort which you foiled?'

Holmes stared at me. 'You are positively incandescent, Watson. And it is a pretty compliment you pay me. But I fear that I must disclaim any responsibility. One may perhaps think that a lofty brow, a distinguished profile, be-token great mental powers, and that a man who looks like me must necessarily think like me; but I imagine that a mere passing resemblance would not go very far with Moriarty. No, his closest associates were chosen on the basis of their intellect, not their good looks!'

'H'mm.' I was reluctant to give up my theory entirely. 'And yet, were there two men with the same intellect, might appearance ... the resemblance to you ... not have been a deciding factor?'

Holmes laughed. 'I can go along with you there,' said he. 'Whatever his testimonials, Moriarty's agent did his work well. As long as Moriarty was alive, of course, the agent was merely a second in command ... although you must remember that even Moriarty could not be in two places at once, and he was usually in London, so that his agent in France had pretty much of a free hand. He was ... and still is ... a clever man, Watson. Clever, bold, and ruthless. Once Moriarty had met his untimely end, then of course the agent took over the Continental operation.'

'As a going concern? Had you not spoiled their sport to a large extent, Holmes?'

He frowned. 'I had hopes that I had frustrated Moriarty's attempts to move his activities across the Channel; but my own small efforts were naturally concentrated on the English side. And even then – for reasons which I had best not dwell upon – the police action left many of the highly placed members of the gang at liberty.'

I nodded. 'I well remember your annoyance on learning of their escape!'

'A justifiable annoyance, I think, under the circumstances. There was devilry in that escape, Watson. A stench of corruption in high places. And ... one day ... there will have to be a reckoning. But you were asking me about France. Even though I did not dare to contact you, I had my channels of communication, and news kept reaching me on my travels of the doings of Moriarty's erstwhile agent. To me, who had studied Moriarty's own methods for so very long, and so intently, the pattern was clear. This latest outrage ...' and he indicated the great pile of newspapers – 'is but the latest, the most audacious, of his crimes.'

I waved one of the newspapers at him. 'But it says here that the assassin was an anarchist! He is known to the police!'

Holmes lifted an eyebrow wearily. 'A motley throng gathers round the red-and-black banner,' said he. 'I have no doubt that some of them are honest enough by their own lights, that they are motivated by what they see as a genuine desire to change the political system. But on the other hand, I know as a fact that many of them are not, that they are merely cynical opportunists with an eye to their own gain. Those with an authentic zeal for change are easily manipulated by the rogues, and I have no doubt that such is the case in this instance. What does it matter that the actual assassin was taken? It was ever thus with the professor. The apparent criminal might be caught by the police, or torn apart by the mob; he might be tried, flogged, imprisoned, or even hanged. But the true criminal, the planner, the man behind the crime, the spider at the heart of the web, he would never be taken. The mark of Moriarty, my boy! Why, you might almost use that phrase as the title of one of your sensational novels! "The Mark of Moriarty!" I recognize the brushwork, Watson. If this is not a genuine Moriarty, then at least it is of his school. And a master pupil at that.' He sat upright. 'Would you be so good as to pass me the Bradshaw, Watson?'

'The boat-train to France?'

Holmes nodded.

'There are obvious difficulties,' I told him. 'For one thing, it is clear that this man of whom you speak knows exactly what you look like ... he could hardly impersonate you so successfully were it not so.'

Holmes shrugged a shoulder. 'After all, our quarry is not the only man to have some experience in acting or disguise.'

'"Our" quarry, Holmes?'

'Well, I thought that perhaps ... if you have nothing better to do ...'

'Not I.'

'It will be dangerous, Watson.'

'So much the better! I cleaned my old revolver just this morning.'

'And it will require some degree of cunning, for we have not the first idea of where to begin our search.'

'After all, Holmes, our quarry is not the only man to have some experience in duplicity, nor yet in thinking fast under fire.'

Holmes laughed. 'Can you be packed and ready in half an hour?'

'I am ready now. But one thing I must insist upon, Holmes.'

'And what may that be?'

'I will not ... under any circumstances ... wear a false beard.'

Three

Holmes and I landed in France at Dieppe, having caught the overnight boat from Newhaven. Not the most direct of routes, and one that probably would not have occurred to me; but Holmes said that he thought it safer, although he admitted that the chances of our being watched or followed were slim.

The casual observer would possibly not have recognized either Holmes or myself when we stepped on to French soil. Before we left 221B, Holmes had used his skills to disguise us both as far as possible. He did not bother with dyes, or with that false beard which I had abjured – indeed, he rather sneered at these things as smacking of the amateur. 'Dyes and glues must be constantly renewed,' said he, 'and even then they may be depended upon only to the extent that they will inevitably let you down at a critical moment. Subtlety, Watson, that is the thing.'

My moustache had been rather in need of trimming anyway and, with a few deft snips of the scissors and the judicious application of a little wax, Holmes had produced a distinctly Continental jauntiness on the upper lip; a suit which I hardly dared to wear in London, a larger and more flamboyantly coloured cravat than I would habitually have affected, together with a glittering fake-diamond pin, bought for ninepence in the Bazaar on the corner, and Holmes could regard me with almost an approving eye. 'One last touch, I think, Watson.'

He rummaged in my wardrobe, and produced a Coke hat, in a style which had gone out of fashion some ten years before, and which had been gathering dust and fighting a losing battle with moths ever since. 'There! An excellent example of the Middle European popinjay,' said he, as he perched the thing squarely on my head. 'Just remember to be rude to the servants, sneer at your betters ... and that, for your information, means just about everyone you will meet ... and always count your change. Twice.'

I must say that if I looked somewhat disreputable, Holmes looked considerably worse. Clad in a shiny black suit, a dirty collar on a dirtier shirt, two-tone shoes with grubby lavender spats, and a gimcrack gilt monocle on a frayed cord, he looked every inch the unsuccessful commercial traveller who has escaped from his wife for a day or so – and who intends to take full advantage of the fact. The crowning glory was a brown felt hat, which spoke of extensive acquaintance with Newmarket Heath, and none at all with good taste.

'For heaven's sake do not go anywhere near Lincoln's Inn,' I advised him, 'or the lawyers will take you for a professional co-respondent looking for work! Whilst if you linger too long near Tattersalls, they will undoubtedly have you warned off the turf as a tout!'

'A second career is always a useful thing,' said he. 'Our disguises are not perhaps the most elaborate, but that is all to the good, as they will not need that constant repair work to which I referred just now. In any event, I have hopes that news of my return to the land of the living may not yet have reached the Continent. But the sooner we assume our new personae the better.'

On the platform at Dieppe, Holmes looked round carefully. 'We have not, I think, been followed,' said he, 'nor are we being watched. But for all that, we must go carefully from this point on, Watson, for we are now very definitely in the enemy's territory.'

We shared our carriage with the usual motley throng, a mixture of French and English travellers. Holmes managed to curl himself up in a corner seat with a bundle of French newspapers, and responded only monosyllabically, and in French or broken English, to such conventional polite remarks as were made to him by the other passengers. I, meantime, settled down with my eyes half-closed, as if dozing after the tedious sea-crossing, and listened as intently as I might to the conversations of my neighbours. As could be expected, the assassination of the President of the Republic loomed large in the various discussions. The speech of the French passengers was indicative of a mixture of anger and disbelief, whilst the English tended to express the pious hope that the event, sad though it undoubtedly was, would not make life too tiresome during their own pleasure-seeking sojourns in the capital.

Having arrived at St-Lazare, Holmes once again studied our fellow passengers as they streamed towards the customs examination. 'All seems in order,' said he. We passed the *octroi*, where Holmes was obliged to pay a hefty impost on account of the vast quantity of tobacco that was found amongst his luggage, and then sought out lodgings in an hotel of middle size and middle class in the Rue d'Amsterdam, at no very great distance from the station. 'Large enough,' said Holmes, after we had signed the register in the names of Mr Harris and Mr Price, aliases which we had used before, 'and cosmopolitan enough that we shall attract no particular attention, and yet small enough for us to keep a wary eye open for possible danger. Moreover, being so near the railway station, they will be perfectly accustomed to guests arriving and leaving at odd hours, so that it is in every way suitable for our plans.'

'Which are?'

'A bath, and a belated lunch, I think, might be indicated. And then we must visit Dubuque, to see if he can point us in the right direction. I have pretty well lost touch with things over here in the last three or four years; such trails as I might once have followed have largely gone cold, so that all we have to go on is this assassination, and the anarchist undertones to it. I have hopes that Dubuque and his fellows may know something more than has appeared in the newspapers.'

After that lunch Holmes had mentioned, we made our way to the prefecture of police, and sought out Dubuque, who was, we were told, in his office. Holmes was about to take out a card, but then thought better of it. 'Would you tell Monsieur Dubuque,' said he to the uniformed *gendarme*, 'that it is in connection with the Affair of the Second Stain?'

The policeman looked puzzled at so odd a request from so shabby a petitioner, but ... perhaps taking us for criminals who wished to inform on their colleagues ... went into Dubuque's office. A moment later, the door burst open, and Dubuque himself came out to greet us. 'Monsieur ...' but before he could say more, Holmes held up a warning finger. 'Ah,' said Dubuque, tapping the side of his nose significantly, 'I comprehend! You are here on business, no doubt? Come in, come in!'

He stood aside to let us into his office, and after telling the still puzzled *gendarme* to bring some coffee, Dubuque closed the door, waved us to chairs, and passed over a box of cigars. 'The policeman, he mentions an Affair of the Second Stain. For a moment I wonder, has he gone mad? But then at once I recollect; I understand that Monsieur Sherlock Holmes and Doctor Watson are here to see their old friend. But I am still puzzled ... why have they left it so long?'

Holmes laughed, and quickly gave Dubuque a somewhat condensed account of the last three years. Whilst he did this, I was at liberty to study the famous Parisian detective and his surroundings. I myself had first made Dubuque's acquaintance at the end of that case of *The Second Stain*, mention of which had proved to be our passport to Dubuque's office ... although I believe that Holmes and Dubuque had worked together earlier, without me. The case I have mentioned had international political ramifications, and Dubuque had been most interested in Holmes's explanations, and most generous in his praise of my friend's work.

At the time of which I am now writing, Dubuque had risen to be one of the most respected of the detectives in the Paris police. He was some forty years of age, with an ornate moustache which put my own in the shade. He was dressed soberly enough, but yet in the height of the fashion, while his waist, slightly thicker than it had been when last I saw him, bore testimony to his love of good food and fine wine.

Dubuque listened spellbound, an unlit cigar between his fingers, whilst Holmes told his tale. At the finish, Dubuque threw the cigar down and clapped his hands. 'Magnificent!' said he. 'You have lived a lifetime … two lifetimes … in the last few years!' And then his brow clouded. 'But now, one has no doubt, you have come to France because of this most dreadful, this intolerable crime?'

Holmes nodded. 'I discern the hand of an old enemy,' said he. 'One whom we pursued together, some four years ago.'

'But the assassin was an anarchist!' cried Dubuque.

'Pshaw! A mere blind!'

Dubuque gave an expressive shrug of the shoulders, and looked at me. 'Monsieur Holmes, he has his own ideas, *n'est-ce pas*? But we have seen his ideas proved right often enough, have we not? And so I say, lead on where you will, *mon vieux*, and you shall see that Dubuque follows close behind.'

Holmes shook the Parisian detective's hand. 'I am delighted to hear you say so. Now, the only clue we have in this affair is this dreadful assassination, and the clear association with the anarchists. I know you of old, Monsieur Dubuque, and so I ask you this … have you, or your colleagues, any spies in the anarchist camp?'

Dubuque looked at Holmes for a long moment before answering, then he stood up abruptly. '*Bien*. You know our methods, Monsieur Holmes. We have maintained a watch on these rogues, and for one or two of them we have a *dossier*. But only for one or two, because they are so cunning. To find out anything significant, it is difficult … dangerous.' He lowered his voice. 'And yes, I have a man in the society, on the inside. He is trusted, so he can introduce you. But you will understand, once you have gained admittance, you will be on your own, you and the good Doctor Watson.'

Holmes nodded briefly. 'That is understood. When may we meet this man of yours?'

'It will be safer for him to meet you, in his own good time. Where are you staying at the moment?'

Holmes told him the name of our hotel. Dubuque jotted it down, then stood up and held out a hand. 'His name is Lefevre,' he told us. 'Or at any rate, that is the name he uses for the moment. But, just as a small precaution, I shall instruct him to mention your own London address,' and he tapped the side of his nose, and gave us a conspiratorial wink.

'By the by,' said Holmes, 'I am Mr Harris, and Watson here is Mr Price.'

'I understand perfectly.'

Holmes and I made our way back to the hotel, there to await the arrival of Lefevre. Holmes paced impatiently up and down the sitting-room, smoking his pipe, the whole afternoon. Rather than do the same, I determined that I would read as many of the French newspapers and magazines that I could lay my hands on, to saturate myself, as it were, in the atmosphere of the capital, and perhaps obtain some information that would prove to be of some assistance in our investigations.

At around seven o'clock, Holmes pulled out his watch for the fiftieth time since we returned to the hotel, and said, 'Dubuque's fellow is evidently in no hurry. I suggest we go to our dinner, Watson.'

'Gladly,' said I, and meant it, for Holmes can be indifferent to food when he is fairly on a case, and all too often he is deaf to my protestations – a circumstance which has led to my acquiring a totally undeserved reputation for gluttony, when in reality I merely try to prevent Holmes's collapsing from hunger, and taking me along with him.

Holmes led the way to the street, and we set off in search of a decent restaurant. We had gone about a hundred yards and were passing a gloomy side alley when a man emerged from the shade and approached us. 'Mr 'Arris, I think?' said he in the most appalling English.

Holmes stopped. 'I am Mr Harris,' said he.

The man held out a grimy hand. 'My name is Marcel Lefevre,' he told us. 'And this, I understand, is Mr Price?'

He insisted on shaking my hand, and I was acutely aware of an odour of *absinthe*, garlic, and the cheap, dark tobacco smoked by the French workman. Lefevre's appearance was very far from prepossessing. He had clearly not shaved for three or four days, and I rather suspected he had not washed in that time either. His clothes were greasy, his boots shabby, and the hand which he held out to me shook, as if with delirium. A moment's thought, however, reminded me that neither Holmes nor I looked particularly like an oil-painting. Lefevre's disguise, for such I now realized it to be, could certainly not be faulted, and accordingly I shook his hand heartily – and was obliged to wipe my fingers on my coat tails afterwards.

'The 'otel, it is nice, yes?' said Lefevre, in a curious sort of broken English which made him sound for all the world as if he were touting for a rival place of business.

'It is adequate,' said Holmes.

'But perhaps I can tell you a better place to stay,' said Lefevre. 'It is a *pension*, you understand, owned by a good friend of mine. I stay there myself, in point of fact. I think it would be better for you, more … *commode* … what do you say? … yes, convenient. Although,' he added in a lower voice, 'it cannot, of course, compare with a suite of rooms at 221B Baker Street.'

'Very well,' said Holmes in French. 'You advise us to move there?'

'Tomorrow morning will be soon enough,' said Lefevre. 'Ask at the hotel for your account to be made up, ready for the morning. You will leave as if you were taking a train, you understand? Now, you know the Collège de France, on the Left Bank?'

Holmes nodded.

'Take a cab. Be outside the Collège at ten o'clock tomorrow morning. Wait there as if you were tourists, seeing the sights. I shall meet you there.' And he nodded briefly, and disappeared back into the shadows.

Holmes and I ate our dinner pretty much in silence, for he refused to answer any of the questions I put to him, saying only that we must be prepared for any eventuality – useful advice enough, to be sure, but hardly constructive, and not even particularly original, as I felt obliged to point out.

On the following morning, we paid our bill and set off as if for the railway station. I may add that our luggage consisted of nothing more than a single bag apiece, so there was no difficulty about carrying that. Once at the station we wandered about a little, then left by the main entrance as if we had just arrived by train. We hired a cab, and were soon crossing the river.

Holmes instructed the driver to halt at the Sorbonne, and we walked the very short way to the Collège de France, where we joined a little knot of sightseers, mostly English, and stared with them at the buildings and the surroundings.

Ten o'clock came and went. The sightseers left, and were replaced by another group. Holmes consulted his watch. 'I trust nothing has happened ... ah! There he is,' and he nodded to the shadows, from whence Lefevre had emerged in his mysterious fashion.

Lefevre nodded a quick greeting, then led the way at a good pace, going south along the Rue St-Jacques. We passed the Law School, and the Panthéon – I reflected that it was odd to see these places, which I had known so well under such different circumstances – and set off down the Rue Mouffetard, with its curious relics of the old Paris known to Rabelais and his drinking companions. Lefevre did not allow us time to gaze about us, though, but plunged into a maze of narrow and rather sordid alleys, finally halting before a door, very much weatherbeaten and the worse for wear, in a tall, shabby, old building.

'Here we are,' said Lefevre. Then, evidently noticing my doubtful expression, he added, 'Cheer up, Mr Price! Its appearance is unfortunate, I know, but you will soon come to like it.'

Lefevre led us inside, and summoned the manager or proprietor – I was not sure just what he might be – from a dark back room. He was a short, stout man of greasy appearance, who did not seem particularly interested in us, though he was keen – nay, eager – enough to take a week's rent in advance. We were not asked our names, or required to produce any form of identification, which was rather in defiance of the French police regulations, I fancy. We did not have a great deal of luggage, and that was soon stowed away. Lefevre, who lodged across the hall, had shown us to our room, and stayed whilst we settled in. 'You had best think of some new names for yourselves,' said he when we were done.

Holmes shrugged his shoulders. 'I shall be Pierre Leblanc,' said he, 'and Price here can be Henri Vert.'

'Mr Green and Mr White?' said I. 'A touch obvious, Hol ... ah, Harris.'

Lefevre grinned. 'But these anarchists,' said he, 'they expect the alias, the nickname. Why, one of my best friends in the society is "The Cat," and we have also "Ugly Jean," and so forth. They will naturally assume your names are false, but they would do that in any event.'

So, Henri Vert I became, for the time being. Holmes suggested that I take a stroll round our immediate environs, to familiarize myself as much as possible with the locality. Meantime, he and Lefevre settled in a disreputable bar, and were soon deep in discussion.

I did as Holmes suggested, and wandered around the maze of grimy streets and alleys, marking, with a view to dinner, such restaurants as did not seem too obviously offensive. Along the way I was offered contraband cigar-ettes, some dubious 'tobacco' apparently grown in Morocco, and several interesting propositions which were mostly of a business nature, although several of the local ladies offered me a range of services, none of which – delightful though they promised to be – seemed entirely appropriate to the task which had brought Holmes and me here.

I soon realized that a couple of hours was insufficient to gain more than a very rudimentary knowledge of the area, which resembled in some ways the East End of London. But I flatter myself that I have a good grasp of basic geography, and had soon fixed the main thoroughfares, such as they were, in my mind, although a lifetime would scarcely be enough to get to know all the little courts and alleyways.

I returned to the bar where I had left the others, to find Holmes sitting on his own, a glass of *absinthe* before him. 'Dreadful stuff, that,' said I, nodding to the glass. 'Rots your boots, as the drill-sergeant at Netley used to say.'

'But it is not without its merits as an *aperitif,*' said Holmes. 'You would not care for a glass?'

'Indeed not! But speaking of *aperitifs,* I have noted a couple of relatively clean places where we might dine, were you so inclined.'

Holmes did not, as he had on so many other occasions, dismiss the mention of food out of hand. Instead he nodded slowly. 'It might be as well to take some refreshment,' said he, 'for we have work ahead of us, and in the not too distant future. This fellow Lefevre proposes to introduce us at the next meeting of his society.'

'Quick work! And when may that next meeting be?'

'This evening,' replied Holmes. 'At half past nine.'

Four

'We are scarcely dressed for the Diogenes Club,' said I
ruefully, looking at my reflection in the flyblown glass.

Holmes laughed. 'Perhaps not, but then the company is
likely to prove somewhat more lively than one would expect
to find at that eminent institution. Indeed,' he added
thoughtfully, 'I am not sure but that it might prove a touch
too animated for comfort. You know, Watson, I have serious
doubts as to the advisability of taking you along this evening.
There are certain to be some spirited exchanges, to put it
mildly.'

'Try to stop me!' I told him.

Holmes slapped me on the back. 'Well said, Watson! By the
by, have you your revolver with you?'

I took the pistol from my pocket to show him.

'Is it loaded?'

'It is not much use otherwise, Holmes!'

'Then you will please unload it, and leave the cartridges
behind.'

'But Holmes ...'

'If you would, Doctor,' said he firmly.

I unloaded the pistol as he asked, not without some
muttered protest, and returned it – now useless – to my
pocket. But I noticed that Holmes slipped three cartridges into
his own revolver before he tucked it out of sight.

'You mentioned some sprightly exchanges, Holmes,' said I, as casually as I could manage. 'Your tone suggested that you do more than just expect some excitement.'

'You absolutely scintillate, Watson. Yes, my boy, I flatter myself that I have arranged one or two surprises. You see,' he went on, lighting one of the rank French cigarettes, 'we need to work fast, and for two main reasons. Firstly, our true identity might be discovered ... my enemies, as you are well aware, know me by sight ... and these gentry do not play by the rules of cricket. Secondly, the assassination of the President may well indicate that their plans are almost come to fruition ... for why should they play so desperate a game otherwise? That being the case, we cannot afford to wait, to ingratiate ourselves with these individuals, as we might have done. We need our own spectacular *coup*, something to bring ourselves to the attention of the ruling council as quickly as possible. That is the only way we might be able to reach the top man, and thus smash the entire gang.'

'And we shall do that this evening?'

Holmes nodded. 'God willing, we shall. There will be some excitement, some confusion. Stay calm, and take your lead from me.'

'But my revolver? If there is trouble, we may have to contend with ... with "The Mouse", or "Ugly Johnny", and the rest of the poisonous crew! May I not at least load a couple of chambers?'

'Certainly not! I do not wish anyone to be shot!'

'Not even the anarchists?'

'Particularly not the anarchists! They ... misguided, even dangerous, though they are ... are not our quarry. They are merely our passport to the real brains behind the various criminal activities which bedevil the country. Criminal activities which already include the murder of the President of the Republic! And which ... and which may yet lead to worse things,' he added, half to himself.

'Worse?' said I, but Holmes would not say any more, and I turned back to the glass, which reassured me that I looked as great a miscreant as any in the Newgate Calendar.

'All done?' said Holmes, consulting his watch.

'I am ready,' said I, and followed him down the stairs and along the street to the little bar.

On the way, I had the uneasy feeling that we were being followed. I glanced behind me more than once, but could see nothing out of the ordinary. The events of the day – and, perhaps more to the point, the prospect of what the evening might bring – had conspired, I told myself, to make me more nervous than is customary with me.

Lefevre emerged from the doorway as we approached. He still betrayed not the least indication of familiarity with soap and water, but he had enlivened his shabby costume with a rose in his buttonhole – a red rose, appropriately enough. I wondered if it might be some secret signal to his fellow anarchists, and whether Holmes and I should not visit the florist's. Before I could put my thoughts into words, Lefevre glanced up and down the road before giving his habitual nod of greeting, then set off without a word, with us at his heels.

I had flattered myself that I had gained some general knowledge of the area that afternoon, but Lefevre led us through streets and alleys of whose existence I was in complete ignorance. In the growing dusk we passed little, ill-lit bars, gambling-dens, and yet more dubious establishments, until Lefevre at last took us into a tiny court, and pulled up abruptly before a door slightly more battered than its fellows.

'All ready?' asked Lefevre.

'Ready,' said Holmes.

I nodded.

Lefevre told us, 'If we are separated ... and, Lord knows, that is likely this evening ... ask for "Marcel" at the *pension*, and you will find me. *En avant!*' He straightened himself, as if to prepare himself for whatever might befall, then pushed open the door. We followed him inside, past an open door which showed us a glimpse of tables and chairs, with some half-dozen men and women sitting around talking. To this day I cannot say if it was a restaurant, or a drinking club of sorts, or just what it might have been. But by the door stood a man in a greasy apron, a waiter, or the owner, perhaps, and he gave a piercing look at Holmes and myself before exchanging a nod with Lefevre.

Lefevre continued down a narrow, dirty passage, and up a flight of stairs which had not the slightest vestige of carpet or paint. We stopped on a little landing, which at first seemed deserted, but then a large, rough-looking man emerged, and planted himself firmly in our path. I wondered if this was Ugly John – his face certainly qualified him for the sobriquet.

'Comrades from Corsica,' said Lefevre, nodding at Holmes and myself.

The large man scrutinized the two of us with some care, then at last gave a grunt of approbation – I think it was Holmes's two-toned shoes which finally tipped the scales – and stood to one side to let us pass.

Lefevre pushed open a door and led the way inside. The room in which we found ourselves was bigger than one might have expected from the premises downstairs – 'deceptively spacious', as the house-agents might well have said – but, large as it was, it was crowded. We were evidently the last to arrive, and there seemed no empty places left, but Lefevre begged a couple of chairs from a man who was acting in some sort as an usher, or steward, and we settled ourselves next to the door. The large man who had inspected us on our arrival came in, closed the door behind him, and sat down near us, and I assumed that the business of the evening was about to begin.

The steward, a fussy, self-important little individual, made his way to the front of the room – for there was no pretence at any sort of platform or stage – to announce the first speaker, 'The comrade from Lyons.'

There were three or four of these speakers, all much alike in appearance – which was sordid; and alike also in style – of which more in a moment. None of them was given his real name. 'The comrade from Lyons' was followed by 'The comrade from St-Germain,' and 'The comrade from Marseilles.' If these styles were geographical descriptions, and not mere *nommes de guerre*, then the anarchist movement was widespread indeed, thought I.

And, indeed, the meeting as a whole seemed to have an air of importance about it. Partly, perhaps, that may have been because the speakers were from such diverse locations, but there was more to it than that. They were attended to with an air almost of expectancy – an air which was most definitely not justified by the content of their speeches, which were alike in being pretty well incoherent.

Such as was intelligible was pretty malignant stuff, most of it. We were exhorted to 'trample the oppressors underfoot,' and to 'tear down the bloodstained banner of slavery,' and God alone knows what else. There were, naturally, a good many references to the assassination of President Sadi Carnot, especially from the comrade from Lyons, where the crime had taken place. These men did not consider it a crime, of course, and the atrocity was discussed in a sort of hideous gloating tone, the 'Yah-boo!' style of oratory which should be thrashed out of a boy at ten or eleven years old. The sole consolation was that these speeches did not last much longer than five minutes. For me, even this was five minutes too long, and I fear that I began to grow restive, and glanced at my watch.

Holmes dug me in the ribs, and at first I assumed that he meant it for a reproach, that he was warning me to try to look more like a committed anarchist, but then he gave a little nod towards the front of the room, where another speaker was taking the floor.

This fellow was a different kettle of fish from the poor flounders who had harangued us up to then. For one thing he was introduced differently, not called 'The comrade from somewhere or other,' but referred to only as 'our main speaker.' Then his appearance was altogether more prepossessing than that of his predecessors. He was tall, cleaner than the bulk of the room's occupants, and well enough dressed, though without any pretence to fashion, or to show – he gave me the impression that he would ordinarily have been very well dressed, but had tailored his coat to suit his company that evening. And, above all, he could speak. There was none of the ranting note of badly stifled anger here, but instead a kind of calm reason which was the worse for the hatred which lurked unseen behind it.

He began by giving us a kind of introduction to the anarchist manifesto, an exposition of the 'ideals' – if that is the right word – of the organization. And I have to admit that it was devilish convincing. He pictured an ordinary man, poorly educated and worse paid, whose gnawing sense of discontent mirrored his constant, gnawing hunger, until discontent turned to anger, anger for his own state and that of his starving children, until the point at which the only possible response was to lash out in a kind of blind, un-reasoning fury. Listening to him, I almost felt ashamed of the contempt I had felt for the earlier speakers. After all, I thought, those 'comrades' had not been to a good school, they did not have three, sometimes four, square meals a day, or any of the other advantages which I and my kind took as if of right.

I have said that I almost felt like that. But not totally. It was not, you are to understand clearly, that I had any sympathy at bottom for anything he said. There was nothing like that about my reaction to his words. But his style of delivery was so good, so damnably persuasive, that you felt as if you were listening to a very clever speaker in your club; it was not that you agreed in the slightest degree with what he said, but that you thought it deserved a proper, a reasoned response – if you had but the wit to think of one. And yet he was not at all out of place in those squalid surroundings, or amongst those villains who – if they were taken at their own account – would have no compunction about committing murder! I remember that I thought that this man would have given the great Mesmer a run for his money.

I listened, pretty well spellbound, for what seemed an eternity – I learned later it was no more than twenty minutes – to that soothing, so reasonable voice, when suddenly he broke off in mid-sentence, as there was the unmistakable sound of a police whistle being blown.

I sat frozen to my chair, but Holmes was on his feet at once, and so too was the large man who had guarded the door. The large man moved towards the door, looking all the while at Holmes with naked suspicion in his eyes.

Holmes gestured towards the speaker, who stood irresolute. 'Quickly!' said Holmes to the large man, 'we must get our comrade away to safety, at all costs!'

The large man paused a fraction of a second, then nodded briefly.

'Keep the crowd away from the door,' said Holmes, 'and we shall attend to our comrade.'

The large man moved away from the door, and into the room. 'One moment, comrades!' he told the crowd, which was now on its feet and inclined to be restive. 'Everything will be taken care of. Quickly, comrade!' he added, looking at the speaker, who had still not moved.

Holmes opened the door, and glanced out. 'Quick, for the love of heaven!' said he.

The speaker moved to the door, and Holmes led the way out on to the little landing. We crossed to the head of the stairs, and Holmes glanced down, then let out an oath which surprised even me.

I looked over his shoulder, and saw Dubuque, of all men, halfway up the stairs with a dozen stout *gendarmes* hard on his heels! In some surprise, I turned to Holmes, but before I could say anything, Holmes had produced his revolver, and fired – once, twice, thrice, and then there was a click as the hammer fell on an empty cylinder.

Dubuque and two of his fellows lay on the stairs, in grotesque attitudes. The rest of the *gendarmes* had fallen back slightly as Holmes fired, but when once they realized that he had no more ammunition they began to press upwards again, but were impeded by the three bodies.

Holmes turned to us, a look of desperation on his face. 'It is useless!' he cried. 'The stairs are blocked!'

The erstwhile speaker did not hesitate. 'This way!' he told us, and pushed open one of the other doors which led off the landing.

All this had happened quickly – much more quickly than it takes to write, or to read, my account – and I confess that I had not the slightest notion of what to do next. Left to my own devices, I should probably have stood at the head of the stairs until the police reached me, but Holmes grabbed my arm and fairly dragged me after him.

I was aware of a confusion in the doorway of the room where the meeting had been held – it seemed for all the world as if the large man and Lefevre had both been trying to get through the door at the same time, and were now both stuck there – and then Holmes dragged me into another room, and threw the door shut. I heard a key being turned in the lock – it was now dark, and there was no lighting in this room – then a second door at the other end of the room was opened, and again Holmes pulled me to it, and through it.

I heard the sound of a bolt being thrown in this second door, and then the man whom I still thought of as 'the speaker', for I had not the slightest inkling as to what his name might be, told us, 'This way!'

We followed him down a short passage, lit only by a grimy window, then into yet another room. This again had a window which our guide threw open. 'Quickly!' he said, and stepped outside. Holmes followed, then I climbed through the window and found myself on an iron balcony of sorts, from which a rusty stair led down to the street – a fire-escape, I suppose.

I still had no time to think about what had happened, but hastily scrambled down after Holmes and the other man, who did not pause when once we had reached the street, but led the way at a run.

We passed through a grimy alley, a vile courtyard, and emerged on to a somewhat broader street, where the man who had been the main speaker paused. 'We must not run here,' he told us, 'for it would arouse suspicion.'

For answer, Holmes pointed up the street to where a couple of policemen were running towards us. 'It looks as if we must run,' said he drily.

Our companion looked baffled for a moment, then turned on his heel, not running, but walking at a fast pace. Back through the courtyard we went, into the alley, but then we turned in a new direction, and plunged into a veritable maze of narrow lanes and squalid streets, keeping up a pace which soon tired me out. I was grateful when at last we slowed down somewhat, and seemed to be entering more respectable surroundings. The speaker suddenly drew up in front of a decent enough looking carriage. 'Please get inside, quickly,' said he.

I confess that I hesitated, but Holmes showed not the slightest indecision. He climbed into the carriage at once, and I followed.

Our new-found friend climbed in last, and gave a peculiar double knock on the roof with his cane, as a signal to the coachman. Off we went at a good speed. I tried to look out of the window, but the blinds were down, and I had no idea as to where we might be heading. We certainly seemed to be taking no short cuts, for once or twice I fancied that we had gone around in a long loop – probably to confuse pursuers, or perhaps to confuse Holmes and myself, I suspected. Neither Holmes nor the erstwhile speaker – and I still had to think of him in those terms, or as 'our new friend,' or something of that kind, for he made not the least attempt to introduce himself – ventured on any conversation, and I kept silent as well.

At length we drew up. Our new friend got down and held the door open for us. 'If you would be so kind,' said he.

Holmes got down, and I followed. We were pretty clearly inside a kind of courtyard, for there were stables no great way off, while the side wall of a large house was not six feet from where we got out of the carriage. Our friend produced a key. 'You must stay here until things have quietened down,' he told us. He unlocked the door, then stood aside to let us in.

I confess that I would have hesitated, but Holmes did not. He led the way inside, and I followed him into a small and plainly furnished entrance hall, looking rather like a servants' entrance, which I suppose it was, since we had entered by a side door. The gas jets were lit, but not turned up, and we stood there, not knowing what might happen, while the man whom I still called 'the speaker,' ludicrous though the appellation now was, for we had scarcely exchanged a half-dozen words since the excitement at the meeting, locked the door.

He put the key in his coat pocket, and when he turned to face us there was a revolver in his hand. 'You will, I am sure, excuse an obvious precaution,' he said. He turned up the light, and motioned towards the door. We went through into a long passage with a flight of stairs at the end.

'If you would please to go upstairs,' he said.

Holmes led the way upstairs.

'You must stay here tonight,' said our host, nodding at a door.

Holmes opened it, and went inside, and again I followed tamely enough. The lamps were lit in here, too, and showed a large and comfortably furnished bedroom.

'There is a cloakroom through there,' said our host, 'but I am afraid you must miss your supper.'

Holmes bowed, and the man left us, locking the door after him. Holmes's first act was to try the door, but it was immovable. Holmes then looked carefully round the room, although I still have no idea what he was looking for – certainly there was no exit of any sort. The blinds were closed, and when we opened them we saw that the windows were barred, and there were heavy shutters outside. Holmes tried the windows, but found that they were nailed shut.

Holmes, who had not spoken since we entered the room, threw himself down in an armchair and laughed. 'I had hoped that we might get a glimpse of our surroundings, but this room has been pretty thoroughly closed up. I imagine that we are not by any means the first guests to be lodged here.'

'You have no clue as to where we are?'

'Well, we are back on the Right Bank … you heard the carriage wheels go over a bridge and the river, of course? And the house tends to suggest that we are in one of the more fashionable quarters.'

'We seemed to take a long time to get here,' said I.

'Oh, that was to put us off the track.' He frowned. 'I have to confess that it worked … would to heaven that I knew Paris as well as I know London, for they would never have fooled me there!'

'I fancy we passed round the Place de l'Etoile, though, Holmes. And I think that it cannot be too far from here, since that was one of the last circular tours that we made before we got here.'

'Indeed? And what makes you say that?'

'Well, we paused before going around, as if there were a good deal of traffic there which had to be negotiated. And I thought ... I may be deluding myself, of course ... but I fancied that some of the street noises were not altogether inconsistent with that area.'

Holmes clapped his hands. 'Well done, Doctor! I missed that, although I can claim that I was occupied with my own thoughts, which were none too cheerful. Which way did we turn, though? Did you mark that?'

'I rather fear I did not, Holmes,' said I, embarrassed. 'It was so confusing.'

'Ah, well, no matter. It does agree with our contention that we are in one of the fashionable quarters ... towards the Bois, perhaps, or not so far from the Champs-Elysées. So, we have done all that we can. It all went off rather well earlier, I thought,' said Holmes.

'The whole incident was staged, of course,' said I. 'Though I did not immediately realize that you were using blank cartridges.'

'The two "dead" *gendarmes* were drafted in from Dubuque's home town,' said Holmes. 'They will return tomorrow, under the most frightful oaths of silence. Dubuque himself ... well, I rather think that the newspapers will carry reports that show his injuries in a very dismal light.'

'I noticed Lefevre making himself a nuisance in the doorway ... presumably that was to stop the rascals escaping?'

Holmes nodded. 'With a little luck, they will all have been arrested, Lefevre along with the rest. They will naturally be kept in separate cells, so none of them will know what may have happened to the others. Lefevre will return to work as his old self, with his old name ... whatever that may be. It does, of course, mean that he is lost to us for the time being, although I am certain that he will be as busy as ever on the outside.

Dubuque and Lefevre were apparently planning to move against that particular anarchist ring in any event, so it all worked very well.'

'Two birds with the one stone?'

'As you say.' He sat up very straight and grew more serious. 'But I told you earlier that I was preoccupied with my thoughts, and so I was. Dubuque is a good fellow, and Lefevre too, from what we have seen of him. But they are out there, and we are in here. It does mean, Watson, that we are now really alone, and in the very heart of the enemy camp.'

Five

'But what do you think will happen tomorrow?' I asked Holmes after he had made his little speech about our being on our own.

He shrugged his shoulders expressively. 'Whatever happens, it is most unlikely to be dull,' was all he said. He curled himself up in the armchair, rather in the manner of a cat, and in a moment he was fast asleep.

To be frank, this devil-may-care fatalism struck me as considerably less than satisfactory. I tried to console myself, to tell myself that Holmes was right to dismiss the morrow – for what could we do about it, locked in here as we were? – and that my best course of action was to get as decent a night's sleep as I possibly could, for I knew that we should need all our wits about us on the next day.

Accordingly, I settled myself on the bed, which was of a softness that could only be called opulent, and composed myself to sleep. It was a long time before I succeeded, however. I was not hungry, for we had dined well, and I had taken the – to me – elementary precaution of providing myself with a bar of chocolate, in case of emergency, and that still nestled, untouched, in my pocket. No, it was rather that my mind refused to be calm, despite my trying to reassure myself along the lines I have just noted. At last, I determined to try to recollect all that had taken place since Holmes and I started out on this adventure together. I recall that I had got as far as Victoria Station when I fell asleep.

I awoke with a start to find Holmes standing over me, a finger to his lips. He had opened the blinds, and, despite the shutters outside the windows, it was evident from the light that it was early morning. Holmes nodded towards the door, and I heard the sound of a key being turned. I fumbled for my revolver, forgetting for the moment that it was not loaded, but before I could take it from my pocket the door swung open, and there stood – of all things – a footman!

I am not being facetious; he was just such a servant as you would expect to find in any grand house in the better quarters of London. He was elderly and of sober appearance, clad in a smart black outfit – he did not exactly wear a powdered wig, but the look on his face was of such grave civility that even a peruke and court dress would not have seemed at all out of place. He made a stiff little bow, and said, 'Monsieur Constantine would be pleased if you would join him for breakfast, Messieurs.'

I glanced at Holmes, fearing some trickery, but he merely shrugged his shoulders, and followed the man out of the room and down the stairs. The windows – magnificent stained glass that would have graced any cathedral – were set too high in the staircase to afford any view of the outside world, so that we still could get no clue as to where we might be. I brought up the rear, keeping a sharp look-out, but saw nothing untoward.

The footman held open a door for us to pass through, and we entered a large, bright room furnished in the style most associated with the fourteenth Louis. A long table was laid for breakfast – the Continental variety, but with a goodly quantity of cold meats and cheese. The man who had made such a profound impression on at least one of his listeners last night, and whose name I now knew to be Constantine – if that really were his name, I thought, and not yet another example of alias or affectation – sat at the head of the table. He waved us to chairs. 'Please, join me,' said he. He indicated the food spread out before us. 'And do not hesitate to help yourselves ... I know you must be hungry after last night's adventures.'

I needed no second urging, for I have always had an excellent appetite, and this particular morning I was indeed ready for something nourishing, whether because of last night's excitement, as Constantine had said, or because I had passed so disturbed a night, I cannot say. I can say that I piled my plate higher than politeness might strictly require.

I was a little surprised to note that Holmes, too, was enjoying his meal like the best of trenchermen, for he is somewhat inclined to forget his stomach whilst involved in a case. Then I bethought myself that he was acting in character. We were, after all, meant to be a couple of rough desperadoes, who did not know when our next meal would be, or from whence it might come. Very well, I could act my part every bit as convincingly as Holmes, and I took a second helping without any prompting.

Constantine himself said nothing whilst Holmes and I ate. He ate little himself, merely making a show of playing with a *croissant* – indeed, now that I think about it, I am convinced that he had already breakfasted before we were released, so that he might observe us the better.

For myself, I had a great curiosity about this man, and whilst I ate my breakfast I in my turn made a point of observing him as best I might, but still trying not to arouse his suspicions. Seen in daylight, he was older than he had appeared in the dim, smoky surroundings of the anarchist meeting, seeming nearer sixty than fifty. Older, yes, but also more muscular than I should have thought looking at him when he spoke to the meeting last night. An aristocratic enough profile and bearing, combined with a tremendous virility, made him a curious sort of compound of the nobleman and the *apache*. If I had to find a comparison, it would perhaps be with one of those hearty aristocrats of the last century, the Regency bucks who raced from London to Brighton with the Prince Regent, or happily went ten rounds with some bare-knuckle bruiser. I should not have cared to meet him in the ring myself, for all that he was twenty years older than I.

What the devil, I asked myself, had such a man as this to do with the rag-tag crowd of anarchists and rogues? As quickly as the question presented itself, the answer came – he was using them, using them for his own ends, which must needs be more villainous yet than anything those anarchists, mere tools, might envisage. This, I thought, might be that spider at the centre of the web whom Holmes had described. Aye, and Holmes and myself fairly in the web to boot!

As I say, the meal was eaten more or less in silence. When we had done, Constantine smiled at us and said, 'Perhaps you would care to go into the next room and smoke a cigarette, to let my fellows clear away in here?'

He got up and led us into a smaller room, furnished in a far more English style, for all the world the sort of private room you might find in a London club. Constantine waved us to chairs, and proffered a silver cigarette box. Holmes helped himself, while I sought and obtained permission to light the ancient briar which I taken with me.

'It is something of a pity that you had but three cartridges,' said Constantine abruptly, when we were settled.

Holmes laughed. He took out his revolver, broke it open, and shook the three empty cases on to his hand. 'One does one's best,' said he. 'Henri here is in an even worse state than I.'

For a moment I wondered who Henri might be, then I recollected myself. I took out my pistol, and displayed the empty cylinder.

'One does one's best,' repeated Holmes. 'But one can do no more … to be frank, Monsieur Constantine, *nous n'avons pas le sou*. When it is all one can do to eat, you understand, little remains for luxuries.'

'I could not help noticing … forgive me, but I could not … that you both had excellent appetites,' said Constantine.

To reinforce the point, I took out my bar of chocolate, held it up, and remarked, 'Dinner. For two.'

Constantine laughed. 'We can perhaps do rather better than that,' said he. He waved a hand to indicate our surroundings. 'What think you to my humble abode?'

I murmured, 'Delightful!' or some such nonsense, but Holmes looked round carefully before he spoke.

'One cannot help but observe that it is slightly different from last night's venue,' said he, with a touch of envy in his voice.

'It is,' said Constantine. He leaned forward in his chair. 'And how do you imagine that I came by it?' he asked.

'Inherited it?' said I.

'Worked for it?' said Holmes, with an undisguised sneer – I have to say that Holmes made a most convincing scoundrel, a perfect compound of the bully and the sneak.

'Two very sensible suggestions,' said Constantine calmly. 'But both are wrong. I inherited nothing, Monsieur ... not even my name, for my mother never knew just who my father was. When I was seven, I was working at Les Halles, sweeping the floors; at twenty, I was chief clerk in a banking house whose name would be very familiar even to you; at thirty I was a director; at forty, governor. In a sense, then, I might be said to have worked for what I have. But you are men of the world, Messieurs ... you know as well as I do that a guttersnipe at Les Halles does not usually rise to be governor of a private bank, however hard he may work. But, you see, I had friends. Good friends, who opened doors for me, made things easier than they might have been.'

'It is a pleasant thing to have friends,' said Holmes. 'Especially good friends.'

'You would perhaps like friends yourselves? Friends who might be relied upon to help you on your way?'

'Such friends might come a touch expensive,' said Holmes thoughtfully.

'Not at all!' said Constantine, lighting another cigarette. 'Hand washes hand. One's friends help out in an emergency; and they naturally rely on one to come to their assistance if it is necessary.' He leaned forward, and studied us intently. 'But tell me, could you see yourself in such a house as this, with servants at your beck and call, with a clear conscience? Might it not conflict somewhat with your anarchist principles?'

Holmes seemed to be considering his response to this, so I said, 'For myself, I have always thought that the redistribution of wealth on a global scale ... though laudable enough in theory ... was an ambitious undertaking. It would be so much easier to begin on a small scale, and redistribute some small portion of it to oneself.'

'Well said!' added Holmes, laughing.

Constantine laughed with him. 'We are of one mind,' said he. 'I will be frank, Messieurs ... I did not attend last night's meeting merely to spout nonsense, but to see whether there might not be there a man, or men, whom I could use in my own enterprises. I believe that you may be the very men I sought. By the by,' he added casually, 'you will not have seen this morning's newspapers,' and he took a couple of newspapers from a table that stood by his elbow, and threw them across to us.

'NEW ANARCHIST OUTRAGE' shouted one headline; and 'TWO POLICEMEN MURDERED: ONE STRUGGLING FOR HIS LIFE!' screamed the other. I glanced over the report – '**Assassins flee justice**,' said one sub-heading; and '**Big police operation**,' another.

'They have a description of the wanted men, you observe,' said Constantine. 'But I do not think that anyone could recognize the two of you from them.'

I looked for the details of which he spoke. Sure enough, there was a lurid and very misleading description of Holmes and myself. Doubtless Dubuque and Lefevre had had a highly amusing time thinking up descriptions of us – descriptions which, I knew well enough, were intended to allow us to move about freely without attracting the attention of such members of the police force as were not in the secret. In that way, the only people we had to fear were the members of the gang – and they were, for me at any rate, more than enough to be going on with.

'It seems that we are safe enough,' said Holmes, with an audible sigh of relief.

'So it seems,' said Constantine, a curious tone in his voice. 'But tell me,' he went on more normally, 'you say you would not be troubled by pangs of conscience to live in a house such as this, to have money in the bank ... to be governor of a bank! But would you truly like to live in such a fashion? It is, I assure you, a very pleasant thing to snap one's fingers ... so! ... and have servants run to do one's bidding. It is pleasant to have good food, fine wines ... beautiful women, perhaps?' he added, looking at me as he said it – though I really cannot imagine why. 'It is agreeable to know that one's pleasures are limited only by one's imagination, I can assure you!'

I have said that he was a persuasive man, and so he was. I knew that he was talking nonsense, that he was preaching greed, and theft, and all the rest of the catalogue of evil. I knew all that. And yet somehow – do not ask me how – it seemed to strike a chord in the innermost darkness of my soul, seemed to appeal to all that was petty and selfish and hateful within me. After all, this man was only doing what many a 'businessman' in the City has done; and at least he was not being hypocritical about it! Yes, thought I, why should I not have some of the good things of life? I had worked hard enough, Lord knows, and for precious little reward! And fought and been injured, too, for an ungrateful country. Did all that count for nothing? Yes; but why should it, when the remedy was within my grasp, there for the taking? There were other thoughts, too, when he spoke of women – darker thoughts yet, thoughts of stories whispered in smoking rooms, thoughts –

At my side, Holmes coughed ostentatiously, and I recollected where I was.

Constantine was saying, 'Well, and does that appeal to you, Messieurs? Would you like to know how it might be done?'

'Just show me the trick!' said I. 'I'll learn it soon enough!'

Holmes was silent for a moment, then he said, 'It might be an interesting change of employment.'

Constantine smiled. 'It might be dangerous.'

'So much the better!' I said boastfully.

'Of course, one does not mind taking risks,' added Holmes, 'if there is some prospect of reward at the end.'

'And it may occasionally be unpleasant,' said Constantine.

Holmes shrugged his shoulders. 'After all, we have neither of us had it particularly easy thus far.'

'And,' said Constantine, 'it may sometimes be necessary to … how shall I say this? … to remove obstacles to one's wishes. To ensure that one's plans are not impeded by officious fools.'

Holmes gave another shrug. 'As you saw last night,' said he carelessly, 'I have no qualms on that score.'

'And our friend here?' said Constantine, staring at me intently.

'I have killed men in my time,' I told him as indifferently as I could – which was true enough in all conscience, though I was in uniform at the time, and acting under orders.

'Well, then,' said Constantine. 'You may be the men I seek. Tell me, though ... can you take orders? Can you act as part of an organization?'

'For myself,' said I, 'I was in the army for some years.'

'Honourably discharged, or ...'

'Honourably, Monsieur!' said I firmly.

'And you?' – to Holmes.

'I can take orders as well as the next man,' said he.

'Are you known to the police?' asked Constantine.

'Not by the names we now use,' said Holmes with a laugh.

Constantine looked steadily at us. 'Then would you like to join me?' he asked in a level tone.

'Indeed, yes,' said I.

'And you, Monsieur?'

Holmes shrugged. 'I shall go along with Henri here. For the moment.'

Constantine sat back in his chair, and took another cigarette from the box. 'I am delighted to hear you say so,' said he. He lit his cigarette, then suddenly leaned forward, all traces of cordiality gone. 'I tell you this ... had your answer been otherwise, you would never have left my house alive! And there is one little thing more, Messieurs. If you play fair with me, I shall play fair with you. You will have money, clothes, women ... all that you desire shall be yours. But if you betray me, if you even think of betraying me ... well, let us not dwell on that! And remember always that the police still want you for the murder of their comrades.'

'But they do not have our descriptions!' cried Holmes, managing to inject a curious mixture of despair and bravado into his voice, as if in very truth he did not care much whether he joined Constantine or not, and saw himself being dragged in against his will. I knew he was acting, of course, but for a moment even I could believe that his rejoinder was genuine.

'Perhaps not,' said Constantine. 'But there are witnesses ... for although some of those arrested last night will face the guillotine, some will not. They will go to prison, but they will still be able to testify against you. Remember that; and remember too that the police are the very least of the dangers you face if you let me down in any way.'

'You have nothing to fear, Monsieur Constantine,' said Holmes, his voice now betraying an almost pathetic desire to please. 'We would not, I assure you, dream of betraying you.'

'And especially not when the rewards of loyalty are so great,' I added, looking round the room.

Constantine laughed, becoming his old, urbane self again. 'You are right, Monsieur,' he told me. 'It is best not to dwell on unpleasantness. But keep in mind always, that your allegiance from now on is to me alone.' He stood up and rang the bell. 'You will forgive the observation,' said he, looking askance at our costumes, 'but you are both in need of a change of linen. If you will tell Georges here ... ' he nodded at the footman, who had appeared in answer to the ring – 'your size in clothes, he will provide what is necessary. I regret that you will not be able to visit the shops for yourselves just at the moment ... it will be much better all round if you remain in the house ... but you may have the utmost confidence in Georges' taste.' And he gave a taut smile, and made a little bow of dismissal.

We followed Georges upstairs to the door of our room. 'If Messieurs would be so kind as to let me have a note of their collar and shoe sizes, and the like?' said Georges, taking out a tiny notebook and silver pencil. We did as we were asked, and Georges indicated the door. 'And if Messieurs would now have the very great goodness to enter their room and remain there? I shall return in a very short time, I assure you.'

We went inside, and Georges shut the door. We heard the key turn again, and Georges' footsteps move discreetly away across the landing.

Holmes threw himself into his armchair. 'We must possess our souls in patience,' said he, 'and trust that Georges' sartorial tastes are not too divergent from our own.'

'Whatever he may choose, it must be better than those hideous brothel-creeper shoes of yours, Hol – er, Leblanc.'

Holmes stretched out his legs, and regarded his feet critically. 'I have rather grown to like them,' said he.

'You know,' said I with a sort of embarrassed half-laugh, 'this Constantine is a most persuasive fellow! Why, I half believed some of the nonsense that he was telling us, if you will credit that!'

Holmes did not laugh at this. He said, very seriously, 'He is undoubtedly an imposing personality; he has, I think, some of that curious "animal magnetism" of which Mesmer and his colleagues speak so highly.'

'He could make a fortune on the stage as a hypnotist, that is certain.'

Holmes did laugh at that. 'But more to the point,' he said, 'he can impose his will on others; he can influence otherwise perfectly ordinary men to evil. That is not such a common trait, and it makes him very dangerous.'

'Tell me, do you think that this is the man we seek? The head of the gang? He has surely the necessary attributes.'

Holmes shook his head. 'No. No, for all that he is a powerful, even an impressive, man, a strong personality. For one thing, he is quite unlike me in appearance … he could never have impersonated me at the Banque de France, as the man whom I know to be the head of the gang did. And then, with all due respect to ourselves, I scarcely think that the head of the gang would recruit new members from the gutter, as it were! Moreover, there was danger in his attending that meeting, a danger which I think the head of the gang would avoid it he could … this fellow Constantine evidently takes a pride in laughing at danger, as he takes a pride in bending others to his will …'

'You almost had me fooled,' I interrupted.

He laughed. 'I thought it as well to show some reluctance at first,' said he. 'That would have been in character, I fancy. And besides, if he thinks we are afraid of him, he will not be quite so suspicious. But you were asking about his position in the gang. It is always possible that he is the leader, but I think it improbable. No, I do not think he is the ultimate head. I fancy that I can see this Constantine as occupying a position similar to that held by Colonel Moran. He is perhaps the chief of staff, responsible to the true leader for the day-to-day business of the organization, for recruiting new members ... like ourselves! You heard him boasting ... he has evidently been dishonest from a youth, or he would not, as he says, have progressed so rapidly.'

'You think Moriarty had connections here that long ago, then? Why, it must have been thirty years ago ... perhaps forty ... that this Constantine started on his upward ... or downward ... path!'

'I think not,' said Holmes. 'I rather think Constantine was already a pretty fair villain when Moriarty ... or the other man, the head of the gang ... found him. You see once again an instance of what I might call the "Moriarty method" ... that is exactly as it was with Colonel Moran, who was already a villain of the deepest dye when Moriarty recruited him. Despite what the natural philosophers would say, in the criminal fraternity like does not repel, but attracts, like. This Constantine was obviously a good catch for the gang ... director of a private bank, but with some flaws in his character ... and, by the way, his being now the governor of a bank might mean that it was he who suggested the attempt upon the Bank of France, although I am certain that he himself was not in the group which made that attempt.' He leaned forward and stared at me. 'One thing I did take very seriously, and that was his threat to kill us if there were the slightest grounds for suspicion. You will recall that Moriarty, too, knew only one penalty for treachery, or suspected treachery ... death! Yes, my boy, we are truly past the point of no return.' He stood up, and strolled to the window. 'I wonder what sort of cravat Georges will buy me?'

'And I wonder just what Constantine has in mind for us.' And I stared into space, unable to think about anything else but our fate.

A

61

Six

Georges was as good as his word. He returned in less than two hours, bearing a couple of large parcels, which he set down on a little table, before bowing gravely to us, and leaving the room. I noticed that this time he did not bother to lock the door.

'Just like your tenth birthday!' said I, nodding towards the door as I spoke.

Holmes quickly inclined his head, to show that he knew the door was unlocked, then just as quickly shook it, to let me know that we were to stay in the room.

I opened the parcels, and we examined Georges' purchases. I could not really fault his choice. The garments he had provided were good quality, but not so expensive as to attract attention. My own outfit was a touch more conservative than the garb I had sported up to now, but was still somewhat louder than I would have cared to wear in Baker Street. When once I had changed, I looked like a middle-class clerk who had just been paid a modest bonus; that, or a businessman slightly, but not significantly, down on his luck. My sole regret was that Georges had not brought us new boots. The ones I had picked to wear on this adventure were respectable enough, though an old pair, and very down at heel – but I could have wished that Georges had brought replacements for Holmes's two-coloured monstrosities. As it was, and despite the fact that I could no longer see my reflection in his coat, I regret to say that Holmes looked more than ever like a professional dancing-partner.

Along with the change of raiment, I took the opportunity to remove the last traces of wax from my moustache, and trim the ends, so that it was back to its old – English – self.

Holmes regarded me critically when I had done. 'They do not know you by sight,' said he, 'so you should be safe enough. But I must continue to act my part.'

And he was as good as his word. How he did it, I frankly confess I do not know. As I say, he would have nothing to do with false beards, wigs, paint and the like, and yet in some mysterious fashion he actually managed to look quite different. I can only attribute it to the fact that Holmes himself was not devoid of that 'animal magnetism' we had spoken of earlier, which some men have in abundance while yet others – like myself – unfortunately do not possess at all.

An hour or so later, Georges came to take us downstairs to luncheon. Constantine was sitting at the table. He regarded us with a certain amount of approval. 'I think that is more satisfactory,' said he. 'After all, one wishes one's associates to look respectable, does one not? Now, please enjoy your meal.'

As before we ate in almost complete silence; and once again Constantine himself ate very little, but merely watched us throughout the meal. Holmes and I made occasional attempts to engage Constantine in conversation, but he made only monosyllabic replies. When we had done, Constantine remarked, 'You will please return to your room. I do not propose to insult you by locking you in, or anything of that sort … you have already had the opportunity to leave, had you wished … but I have callers this afternoon, and I do not wish you to see them. And, equally to the point, I do not wish them to see you. I am sure you will understand.'

We nodded our understanding.

'Georges will bring your dinner to your room this evening,' Constantine went on, 'for again I shall have other guests. And then when once it grows dark, Georges will set you on your way to your lodgings … you had best give me the address.'

Holmes did so, and Constantine said, 'You will remain there tomorrow morning, if you please, and I shall send an emissary … he will mention the name "Jean-Paul". You will obey him in all respects, as if it were me speaking. And now I must say farewell. As I say, I have engagements for the rest of the day, and you will be gone before I am free again. But … if you make good progress within our little family, as it were … we shall meet again before so very long.'

'And if we do not make good progress?' asked Holmes.

Constantine smiled. 'Ah … I fear that in that event, we shall not meet again. But let us not think about that very disagreeable prospect.' He held out his hand. '*Au revoir* … that is, let us hope most sincerely that it is *au revoir*.'

Holmes shook his hand. 'I am certain that we shall meet again,' said he.

We returned to our room, where Holmes yet again curled himself up in his armchair. 'I would to heaven we might catch a glimpse of this afternoon's visitors!' said he. 'It might have told us a good deal. But I fear we simply do not dare to make the attempt … Georges, or one of the other servants, is sure to have been told off to keep an eye on us.' And he lapsed into a sort of brooding silence which I did not feel inclined to disturb.

The afternoon seemed to me to drag intolerably. I could not tell if Holmes was asleep – if he was not, then he was so immersed in his own thoughts that he was as insensible of the outside world as any Indian fakir on his bed of nails. How I wished that I had brought a book to read, or paper and pencil to play noughts and crosses with myself, anything to break the monotony. But then of course I had not imagined that I would be a bird in a gilded cage! Holmes now seemed to be asleep, and I got up and started to wander quietly around the room.

There was a chest of drawers by the bed, and I opened the top drawer. It was empty, as was the next. But in the bottom drawer I found – concealed under some socks and handkerchiefs – a little book, nicely bound in vellum but with no title on the spine. Someone had put a piece of paper in, evidently to mark their place, and naturally enough I opened the book at that point. The book itself was a profusely illustrated work of the variety which booksellers label *curiosa*, or *facetiae*, and was very definitely 'privately printed in Paris.' If it were Constantine's, then it certainly threw an interesting light on his tastes; while if it belonged to Georges, then that seemingly impeccable servant would go down greatly in my estimation.

There was nothing to be made of the book, so I took out the marker, and glanced at that. It was a half-sheet of notepaper, the top half evidently, for there was some sort of a crest at the head of it, and a date '16 April' – but no year – and the superscription, 'My dear Constantine,' both written in a sort of hasty scrawl. But then the rest of the letter, if letter it had been, had been torn off and discarded. I turned it over, and on the back was that most prosaic of things, a laundry list – 'five silk shirts, eleven collars' and so forth. Still, it might be a clue, and I put it down carefully, intending to show it to Holmes, or to study it more intently myself, later. To pass the time – and for no other reason, I assure you – I actually started to read the book, but Holmes stirred in his chair, and, just as the previous reader had done, I hastily stuck the bit of paper in to mark my place, then put the book in my pocket.

Holmes looked at his watch. 'It will soon be time for our dinner,' he told me.

'I had not realized it was so late. Tell me, Holmes, what do you think this fellow Constantine has in mind for us?'

'Well, it is clear that we are to join his band of brigands, is it not?'

'Oh, I had worked that much out ... but I meant rather that it is surely a step backwards for us, so far as our investigation goes, that is. After all, by encountering Constantine, we have started almost at the top, as it were. If we are now reduced to the ranks, obliged to start picking pockets, or scrumping apples, then we have surely lost that initial advantage?'

Holmes laughed, then considered this more seriously. 'I see your point, and in fact it is something which had already occurred to me. But I confess that I cannot see any quick way round it ... we can hardly presume upon our very slight acquaintance with Constantine to ask for an introduction to his master, now can we? No, we must possess our souls in patience ... or as close to it as we can manage ... and hope to show our worth as more humble members of the gang. And thereby, of course, progress up the ladder, and perhaps catch sight of the real head of the gang. Now, that is my plan at the moment; but if that proves too tiresome, then I suggest that we might make good our escape, slip out of sight and try to find this house, and then follow Constantine wherever he leads us, in the hope that he will take us to the man we seek.'

'It is a gamble, either way,' said I doubtfully.

'I quite agree with you. But, as I say, to press the matter, to ask to talk to Constantine's chief, would arouse suspicions. No, let us see what befalls, let us give it a reasonable time ... shall we say a week or so? After that time, if we are no further, we shall resume our own identities, and try to track Constantine, and, through him, the head man. Detective work is, I fear, sometimes a tedious business. You saw that for yourself in that little affair at Baskerville Hall, where you had days, or even weeks, of inaction, and then everything happened more or less at once. And my own investigations into Moriarty entailed more days ... and nights ... of fruitless, boring watching, with very often nothing to show at the end of it all. But, in the end, it was worth it. Naturally, your readers know little of this; they think it is all excitement, a continuous succession of rousing events, because you can gloss over the more pedestrian elements, dismiss weeks, months, years, in a couple of lines or paragraphs.'

'It will not be years, I trust,' I said with a laugh. 'And I hope that I am as patient as the next man. But is there not a case to be made out for slipping away now, contacting Dubuque, and having Constantine arrested?'

'A bird in the hand, you mean? There is always an argument for immediate action, Doctor. But in this instance, I really think it would achieve very little. For a start, on what charge could Dubuque arrest Constantine? All we know against him is that he spoke at an anarchist meeting ... even if we could establish that to the satisfaction of a magistrate, for Constantine is sure to have provided himself with an alibi, so it would be our word against his, and that of his friends, who are sure to be directors of banks, and what have you, just as he himself is. In England, our word might count for something, but here ... well, let us say that it would be difficult. For the rest, again there would only be our word for it that he offered us membership of a criminal organization ... we might well simply be laughed out of court, if the matter even actually got that far. If the case against him did happen to hold up, we should have one bird in our net ... a fine, plump bird, I agree, and the world would be better for his having his wings clipped ... but the others would fly off, you may be sure. At the very least, by joining the gang, by getting to know the lesser members, we might be able to take them, or some of them, in our net, too.' He broke off and sighed.

'The prospect seems to bring you little cheer,' said I.

'To labour our ornithological metaphor, I am worried lest our catch should prove to be only a couple of sparrows and finches. The eagles ... or perhaps vultures might better describe them ... might break through the mesh.'

'As happened with the Moriarty gang?'

'Exactly as happened with the Moriarty gang,' replied Holmes. 'The bulk of the gang was taken, sure enough, but Moriarty and three of his closest associates escaped. Moriarty is gone now ... thank heaven! ... and Moran is under arrest, but there are two still at large. And, had they been just a touch cleverer, a touch quicker off the mark, Moriarty and Moran might still be at liberty. That is what I fear, Watson ... that any police action will miss the really important men. I have seen it happen before. And that is why I am prepared to wait, to see just what happens. If at all possible, I want the man who heads this gang, the man to whom Constantine and his like report. If taking that man entails some of the smaller fry going free, then that is a price worth paying. Let us at least give it a couple of weeks, shall we?'

I nodded. 'Put like that, of course I am ...' and I broke off as Georges tapped on the door. 'I am with you!' I told Holmes in an undertone, as Georges entered with our dinner on a silver tray.

The dinner was excellent, and I made a hearty meal, for I reasoned that it might be a good while before we ate anything of this standard again – indeed, it might be a long time before we ate anything, if events started to move quickly. Holmes seemed at first inclined to be up to his old tricks, and merely toyed with his food, but after I repeated his own words to him, that we could do nothing for the moment, but were playthings of Fate, so to speak, he laughed, agreed with me, and ate almost as well as I. When we had done, Georges brought coffee and a couple of excellent cigars – say what you will about Constantine, his hospitality could certainly never be faulted – and we smoked in silence for a time.

When it was late enough to be dark outside – Georges had lit the lamps, for the windows were still shuttered and we could not see for ourselves what the day might be like – Georges appeared, wearing a cloak, despite the fact that the evening was close. 'If Messieurs would be so kind?'

We followed him out of the room. He did not take us to the main stair, but instead led us through a green baize door and down the servants' stairs, until we reached the side entrance we had used on our arrival. Outside, it was beginning to get dark. The carriage stood waiting for us, and we set off at a smart pace.

As before, the blinds were down. Holmes casually moved as if to glance out of the window, but Georges politely but firmly prevented this. And, just as before, we took a very roundabout route. I did my best to listen for street noises and the like and to mark the direction we were taking, and once again thought I could recognize the Place de l'Etoile – but I may simply have been fooling myself that I knew Paris better than was, in fact, the case. Certainly, that was the only landmark I thought I could speak to, and after that I was completely lost. After an hour or so, the carriage drew up, and Georges got down. 'Messieurs?'

We descended into the street. 'You recognize your surroundings?' asked Georges.

Holmes looked round quickly. 'The Halle aux Vins, I think? We are at no great distance from our *pension*. My thanks, Monsieur.'

'I regret that I cannot take you further,' said Georges with a bow.

'No matter.'

'It has been a pleasure to serve you, Messieurs.'

Holmes bowed in his turn. 'The service was faultless.' He stretched, like any cat. 'It is good to taste some fresh air, is it not, Henri?'

'It is indeed,' said I.

Holmes took out a cigarette and lit it in a leisurely fashion. Georges remained, immobile, by the side of the carriage. I could see the badly concealed frustration on Holmes's face. 'Well,' said he at last, when it was obvious that Georges had not the least intention of moving before we did, 'we must bid you good night.' He tipped his hat to the coachman, bowed again to Georges, and set off down the road. At the turning he glanced back. I did the same, and saw that Georges still stood there, unmoving.

'Suspicious devil!' said I. 'He evidently thinks we would follow him!'

'And he is right!' said Holmes with a laugh. 'It would have been unforgivable to have neglected so elementary a clue. But these men are not fools ... Georges has been told not to return if there is the slightest suspicion that we are following. Still, we may console ourselves with the fact that we know something of Constantine ... that he is well to do; that he lives on the Right Bank; and that his house is perhaps not too far from the Place de l'Etoile.'

'Well, that certainly narrows it down quite considerably!' said I.

'And we know his name ... unless it is an alias, which I strongly suspect will prove to be the case. Still, Dubuque or Lefevre may find that out for us.'

We reached the *pension* and Holmes leaned over the little counter, and whispered to the proprietor, 'I was told to ask for "Marcel".'

The fellow shrugged indifferently. 'Monsieur Marcel, he is in your room.'

'Indeed?' Holmes ran up the stairs, and then stopped. He put a finger to his lips, then produced his revolver from his pocket, indicating that I should do the same. Although we had no cartridges between us, I think that we looked a fine pair of rascals as Holmes pushed open the door and strode inside.

Lefevre, or Marcel, or whatever his real name may have been, was sitting unconcerned in our best chair. I have to say that I should probably never have recognized him, were I not expecting to see him, for – although he was not in Holmes's league in the matter of disguise – he had altered his appearance quite considerably, and now looked like a man of leisure, a man about town.

'You've come up in the world!' said I.

'Ah, Dame Fortune, she 'as smile upon me, no?' said Lefevre in his villainous English, adding in French, 'But how delighted I am to see you, my good friends! I assure you that I have searched every edition of the newspapers most anxiously, expecting at any moment to hear news that two bodies have been found in the river! Tell me, have you met with the same good luck as I myself?'

'We have,' said Holmes. 'Do you know anything of a Monsieur Constantine, around sixty years of age, with something of an aristocratic bearing, but of humble origins? He is the governor of some private bank, but I cannot tell you just which. And his house is on the Right Bank.'

'Near the Place de l'Etoile, or so we believe,' I added.

Lefevre shrugged. 'The name means nothing, I fear. But I shall look into it, you may be sure. You have, I take it, infiltrated this gang?'

Holmes nodded. 'We are to remain here,' said he, 'and wait for this Constantine, or one of his fellows, rather, to get in touch. I have no clue as to what they propose to do with us, but I shall keep you informed. Do you stay here still?'

'I have given up my room here, delightful though it was. But the proprietor can always reach me. You may trust him, for he … well, let us say, he knows who his friends are.' Lefevre stood

71

up. 'I shall find out what there is to know about this Constantine, you may rely on me.' He bowed to us, and left.

I was tired out. The excitement of the previous evening, and the strain of the day – for, although we had done nothing all day, the waiting had tired me more than any amount of action – conspired to make me seek my bed, and I was asleep almost before my head touched the pillow.

When I awoke, the daylight was streaming in through the open shutters, and Holmes was already up, dressed and shaved. We went downstairs, and set off for the nearest café. As we went along, I noticed an ordinary-looking man emerge from a doorway and wander along behind us.

'I believe we are being followed!' I told Holmes in an undertone.

'I spotted him,' he answered. 'It is probably just a customary precaution.'

'Ah, but on the part of whom?' I wanted to know.

We reached our café and ordered coffee and rolls. The man whom I had seen earlier, and suspected of following us, came over to our table, and leaned over to us.

'Monsieur Jean-Paul, I believe?' said Holmes.

A quick shake of the head answered him. 'No, but Jean-Paul has sent me. When you have finished, Messieurs, if you would follow me?'

Holmes quickly drank his coffee. 'Ready, Henri?'

'Perhaps another *croissant*? Oh, very well.' And I followed them outside.

Our guide led us along the road for a hundred yards, then turned into a narrow alley. A couple more turnings took us into ever narrower and ever grimier courts, until our guide halted before a door whose peeling paint was only held in place by a thick coating of greasy dirt. 'Messieurs?' and he stood back to let us enter.

Seven

I followed Holmes into a tiny *bistro*, very dirty and with a thick pall of smoke in the air which set me coughing. A dozen men and women, all as dirty as the place itself – or dirtier – were seated around greasy tables, and as we entered they regarded us with lacklustre eyes, before going back to whatever conversations we had momentarily interrupted. Our guide followed us inside, and nodded his head to show that we were to follow him. He led the way through the little room, pushed open a door in the far side, and took us down a short passage before opening a second door, and motioning us inside.

The room we entered was even smaller than the main bar, and even smokier – perhaps that was as well, for the fumes did serve to obscure the more deep-seated grime which, I felt certain, lurked beneath the shoddy furnishings. The place looked for all the world like some thieves' kitchen straight out of Dickens. Five or six men stood or sat around the room, all smoking, and none of them looking like the sort of man you would meet in the club – or would want to meet in a dark alleyway, for that matter.

One of the fellows stood up, and lounged over to us. 'Jean-Paul,' said he briefly, by way of introduction.

'Pierre, and this is Henri,' said Holmes.

Jean-Paul looked us up and down in an insolent fashion. He gestured at Holmes's shoes. 'We do sometimes need the services of a gigolo,' he said with a leer.

'I shall do my best to measure up,' said Holmes calmly.

The fellow stared at me in my turn, then gave a dismissive shrug. 'And as for Henri here ... well, we always need more brawn.'

'My experience of women ... ' I began hotly, but Jean-Paul silenced me with a rude gesture.

'You are not here to discuss women, *mon ami*, but to take orders from me,' he told me.

'Well, I am ready enough for that!' said I. 'What orders have you? Command me, and you'll see soon enough what I can do!'

He looked at me with a touch more favour than he had shown thus far. 'You are ready to join us?' he asked.

'That is what we are waiting for ... the reason we are here,' I said, while Holmes stifled a yawn, as if he were being kept waiting unnecessarily.

Jean-Paul inclined his head. 'Fine words,' said he. 'We shall see if you can live up to them.' He reached into a pocket, and handed Holmes and myself a silk scarf apiece. 'You know what these are for?' he asked.

Holmes shook his head, whilst I strove to think of the French word for *thuggee*.

Jean-Paul sighed, and demonstrated how to knot the scarf so that it looked for all the world like an ordinary article of apparel whilst round the neck, but could be drawn up quickly over the mouth and jaw so as to form an impromptu mask. 'Got that?' he asked us. 'Right! Come along!' and he pushed past me, and led the way through the *bistro* and into the alley.

'Where are we going?' I wanted to know, but Jean-Paul did not reply until we had reached a fairly busy road. He halted in a doorway, and nodded across the street, where a little post office stood.

'You are armed?' asked Jean-Paul.

I showed him my revolver, under cover of my jacket, and Holmes did the same.

'Loaded?' asked Jean-Paul.

'Not mine.'

'Nor mine.'

Jean-Paul handed us two cartridges each. 'Try not to shoot anyone, unless you have to,' he told us.

'And suppose we need to shoot more than twice?' I wanted to know.

Jean-Paul used a rude expression which was intended to convey the sense that such a prospect did not bother him too much, if, indeed, at all, then led the way across the road. He pulled up his scarf to hide his face, and Holmes and I did the same.

Jean-Paul shoved open the door of the post office, and waved his revolver in the air. 'Keep quiet, all of you!' he roared to the astonished customers and clerks. And to Holmes and me, 'Don't just stand there! Help yourselves, you numskulls!'

I saw Holmes taking cash from a drawer. It was not my part to spoil the performance, I thought, and accordingly I too pulled open the nearest drawer, and grabbed whatever was in there.

Jean-Paul, standing at the door, shouted, 'Quickly! The police!'

Holmes ran to the door, and I followed him. As we reached the door, one of the customers, an elderly and respectable businessman, made as if to attack us with his rolled-up umbrella. I fired a shot over the man's head; while Holmes – a better marksman than I – shot the umbrella out of his very hand! The elderly gentleman made use, I regret to say, of some very ungentlemanly language as he rubbed his arm.

Jean-Paul looked round as we fired, then set off at a run down the street, with Holmes and me hard on his heels. We attracted some odd looks, but there was no attempt at pursuit that I could see. Jean-Paul turned into an alley, and slowed down. He pulled the scarf from his face, and adjusted it, so that he looked as respectable as was possible. He grinned happily at us. 'That wasn't half bad, was it?' said he.

'You could have warned us what you planned!' I grumbled.

'Ah, but I wanted to know how you would react to the unexpected!'

'I saw no police, either!' I told him.

'Well, it was time to go anyway! You didn't do half bad, I must say.' And he led us back to the little *bistro*. The back room was empty – the others were evidently out on business, as it were – and the smoke was starting to clear.

'Now,' said Jean-Paul, lighting a cigarette, 'let's see what we have.' He cast a critical eye over Holmes's booty. 'Cash, is it? Big notes, too! That's not half bad! And a handful of *mandats*. Well, we can make use of those. And good old Henri here has got ... yes, I see it's a sheaf of stamps. Two-centime stamps.'

'I could have done better had I had more warning!' said I. 'Anyway, you can use these when you next write a letter!'

'*Merde*, so I could!' said Jean-Paul with a great roar of laughter. 'That is, if anyone had ever bothered to teach me to write!'

'Oh,' said I. 'Please forgive me ... I could not have known ... look here, Jean-Paul, if ever you need to write to anyone, just say the word.'

Jean-Paul looked at me intently. 'Would you? I have often wished ... my old mother, you know ... in the country ... she worries about me ... and I did promise ... but, well ...'

'Any time,' said I, embarrassed at this entirely unsuspected show of emotion. 'Just tell me what you want to say, and ... well ... we have plenty of stamps, anyway!'

To my horror, Jean-Paul grabbed me. I thought for a moment that he intended to kiss me, but he settled for a hug like the embrace of a grizzly bear. 'You're a good fellow, Henri,' he told me. 'And you're not half bad either, Pierre. Let's have a drink!'

'Shall I ask the owner for a bottle of red wine?' I asked.

Jean-Paul made a rude noise. 'That dishwater?' I paraphrase slightly; he did not actually say 'dishwater' – he was something of a rough diamond, though his heart was undoubtedly in the right place – but 'dishwater' conveys the general meaning of what he did say. 'No,' said he, 'I have some good stuff here,' and he took a bottle from a tall cupboard, and poured us each a generous measure.

As I say, his heart was in the right place, but if that was his 'good stuff,' I dread to think what the bad might have tasted like. Jean-Paul had evidently acquired a liking for it, though, and he helped himself to another glass.

'And then perhaps we ought to think about dividing the spoils?' suggested Holmes, waving a hand at the loot spread out before us.

'Ah.' Jean-Paul looked as nearly embarrassed as was possible for him. 'The thing is ... I know that you took all the risks, and all that sort of thing ... but ... well, that isn't the way it works with us. Everything goes into the kitty, you see, and the lads ... me, too ... we get a regular wage at the end of each week.'

Holmes looked astonished at this. 'But then one might just as well be working in a factory, or behind a desk!'

'No, no,' said Jean-Paul. 'It's not that bad, I assure you. You can work your own hours, more or less; so that if you really want a regular job, you might take one, and do this part-time, as it were. And then there's the bonuses.'

'Bonuses?'

'If there's a big job, you see ... you get a bonus, according to how much work you put in to it, how much risk you took, that sort of thing.'

'A proper fixed scale!' I muttered.

'You have it,' said Jean-Paul. 'And I can tell you that those kind of big jobs come up pretty frequently ... far more often than you or I alone could manage. The chief sees to that. So, you get a bit extra, even though you may not have to do any work! Not half bad, is it?'

'The chief? You mean Monsieur Constantine?' said Holmes.

Jean-Paul looked round anxiously, even though the place was deserted. 'We don't bandy names around too much in here,' said he. 'Most of the lads prefer a nickname, in fact.' He glanced at Holmes's shoes. 'I think we'll have to call you "The Fancy Man".'

Holmes gave a mirthless grin. 'I knifed the last man who made a slighting remark about these shoes,' he said.

Jean-Paul looked at him with a new respect. 'No offence,' said he hastily. 'Have another drink! No, I see it's empty ... never mind, we'll try another bottle,' and he reached up into the cupboard as he spoke. 'Now, about this money … I'm told you're both down on your luck just at the moment, so I'll give you a small advance.' He picked some notes from the heap that lay in front of him, and handed them to us. 'Mind, now! This is nothing more than an advance, and it'll be deducted from this week's wages … I may not read or write as well as you fellows, but I can reckon up all right! Well, that's settled. Drink up, and we'll have another!'

'You were saying about Monsieur Constant … about "the chief", that is to say?' asked Holmes casually, accepting another glass.

'No, no. He … the man you mentioned, he isn't the chief,' said Jean-Paul, refilling his glass.

'No?'

Jean-Paul shook his tousled head. 'Not a bit of it! Just a glorified foreman, same as me, if the truth be known. The chief, he's another thing altogether … you wouldn't want to cross him, I can tell you! Not that you'd want to cross the other one either, but the chief, he's worse.' He glanced around the empty room yet again, and grew confidential. 'Known him for years, me. From the very start.' He glanced round again. 'In the old days, we called him "The Boulevard Assassin". But nobody dares call him that now, I can tell you!'

'And why did anyone call him that?' asked Holmes in an off-hand tone. 'It seems even more droll than "The Fancy Man", when all is said and done!'

'You wouldn't think that if you knew him,' said Jean-Paul. 'As for the name … why, he's a man about town, a *boulevardier*, a real gent. Coat of arms, and all that, one has no doubt. But a killer, too, and there's certainly no two ways about that. I've caught a glimpse of him two or three times … no more than that, in all these years! … but he was always muffled up, a scarf round his chops so's you couldn't see his face properly, but you could see his eyes.' He shuddered. 'Weird, dead eyes. No … what's the word? … no emotion. Like those things … what do you call 'em? With dead eyes?'

'Camel?' I suggested. 'They have strange eyes …'

'A camel? *Merde, non!* A shark! That's what I meant to tell you ... eyes just like a shark! And he'd rip your belly open just as easy, too.' He lowered his voice yet further. 'They say he's killed a dozen men ... maybe two dozen ... with his own hands! Well, you'll say the dogs always exaggerate, and that's true, they'll say anything ... but, with him, I could believe it.'

'But you never saw his face?' asked Holmes casually. 'You do not know his name, let us say?'

The thought seemed to horrify Jean-Paul. He took a long pull at his glass before answering. 'Not I! If I had seen him, or could guess his name, I tell you, I wouldn't be around to talk about it! He is a man who guards his privacy, I can tell you! And he knows everything! Indeed, I think he must be in league with the devil ... that is, if he is not the very devil himself! You can be sure that he will take a look at you ... but you'll never see him!'

'What, he visits here? And in disguise?' asked Holmes.

Jean-Paul shrugged. 'Maybe. Who knows? All I can tell you is he knows everything that goes on here.'

'And he runs the whole show?' asked Holmes. 'For all the world as if it were his own little business? A private army?'

'It is, isn't it?' Jean-Paul looked round again before continuing, 'Don't kid yourselves, though! There's a lot more to it than this den of cheap crooks! Plans, big plans ... that's what the chief's got, big plans. Why, I shouldn't be surprised if one day he wasn't ... wasn't ...'

'President?' suggested Holmes.

'And why not? Look at Napoleon! He started off an ordinary soldier, didn't he? Took over the whole of Europe ... and would've taken over the rest, if he hadn't had the devil's own bad luck!'

'This chief of yours ... ours, that is ... he sees himself as another Napoleon, does he?' said Holmes dreamily. 'I'm surprised he didn't make a move when the President was assassinated a couple of weeks ago.'

Jean-Paul laughed. 'Some silly beggar jumped the gun, didn't he? The chief was mad as hell about that, I can tell you! These damned anarchists ... who can control them? The chief would like to, I can tell you! But they go their own way, half the time.'

'It wasn't in his plan, then?'

'Not a bit of it! Not that I saw him, of course, but Monsieur Constantine, he came here as usual to give me my orders, and he was shaking like a leaf! I'm not kidding ... shaking like a leaf, after what the chief had said. Just as well for that damned fool that the crowd got him first, I can tell you.' He straightened his back, and rubbed his eyes. 'But I'm talking too much! That's dangerous! *Merde*, but I'm drunk!'

'*Merde*, but you are!' agreed Holmes. 'And, in that event, another drink will not do you any more harm ...'

'No, no. It's kind of you, but no.' Jean-Paul shook his head vigorously, as if to clear the fumes from it. 'I have to go ... got to see a man about a dog. Now, my lads, this is how it works with us. You can find this place again, yes? Right. You're to be here each morning at nine ...'

'So early?' I asked incredulously.

'Like your sleep, do you? *Tant pis*! Nine o'clock, on the dot, I assure you! And every day, you comprehend? If you're not here on the dot, it's docked from that week's wages! Now, there may be a little job, and again there may not. If there isn't, then the rest of the day is your own. Stay out of trouble if you can, and if you can't, then don't look to us for help ... we look after our own, right enough, but only when they're acting on orders, understand? And if you fancy a little work on your own account, that's fine ... but remember to tip up any proceeds. Everything goes into the kitty, like I say.'

'But that gives one very little incentive to act on one's own account, surely?' said Holmes.

Jean-Paul nodded. 'That's right enough. But, you see, the idea is that the lads don't act, except on orders from the chief, or ... or the gentleman whose name we won't mention ... or even me, as a last resort. That way, you see, things are more tidy, like; everything can be kept in good order. And then you lads make sure and stay pretty much out of trouble ... as much as is reasonable, that is ... because our jobs are properly organized so's you won't be caught, see? The only danger to you is if you act on your own, and get caught! Now, Saturday's pay day. You'll get a little something, even if you've not done a stroke all week. If you have, like I told you, there'll be an extra bonus, depending on what you did to earn it. If you want to compare pay packets with the others, that's between yourselves, but if they won't tell you how much they've got, I wouldn't press the matter, or you'll more likely get a knife in the ribs than an answer! I don't tell anyone what anyone else has got, I assure you ... and I don't tell 'em what I've got, either! If you think you've not got as much as you deserve ... taking into account the weeks when you got paid, but didn't work, you don't squabble with anyone else, right? You come and see me ... and if you're still unhappy after that, I'll ask Monsieur Constantine to resolve the difficulty. He's ... what's that the shyster lawyers say?'

'"A court of final appeal"?' I suggested.

'Yes, just so. Although you might as well say, "a hanging judge", because you don't want to cross him, even if he is only Number Two. Now, clear off out of here, but be sure to be here at nine tomorrow, and no mistake!' Holmes led the way outside and looked up and down the alley, under cover of lighting a cigarette, before setting off at a stroll. He did not say anything until we had reached a busier street, and were able to find a spot where we could see anyone who approached, but could not be overheard ourselves.

'I do not think we have been followed,' said he, 'but it is as well not to run any risks. We must ask Lefevre if he has found out anything about this fellow Constantine, but then I think we must avoid any further contact with the official forces, unless it is absolutely necessary. What think you to Jean-Paul yonder?'

'He seems a decent enough chap. A bit rough-cut, of course, but a heart of sterling silver, if not exactly solid gold. Reminds me a bit of "Froggy" Mortimer, who was Captain when I was in the First Eleven at school. Fast bowler. "Froggy", that is, not me ... I was always more of a stone-waller, of course.'

'That is really most interesting. And I suppose this youthful amphibian friend of yours is now a senior clerk in some Government office, like that other fellow ... "Tadpole"

Somebody-or-the-other ... whose craving for a cup of cocoa caused him to mislay a valuable treaty?'

'Not a bit of it! Last I heard, old "Froggy" was doing ten years penal servitude, as a result of some very shady dealings on the Kaffir Circus. Biggest crook out! I told you, this fellow reminds me of him.'

'Ah.'

'It is all highly organized, though, Holmes.'

'It is indeed. I need hardly tell you who was responsible for that!'

'Indeed not! But tell me ... do you take seriously Jean-Paul's suggestion that this mysterious "chief" actually comes to that sink of iniquity and spies on his minions?' I asked.

'Well, I do not entirely rule the possibility out. As we have just observed, the gang is run very much on the same lines as the Moriarty gang ... one central, controlling power which directs pretty well all the activity, even what one might call the day-to-day running of the organization. I have no doubt that that central power has its finger on every pulse.'

'But there may be dozens of men in the gang!'

'Hundreds, more like,' said Holmes coolly. 'But remember that so too did the Moriarty gang have hundreds of members, yet the professor knew them all. Oh, he obviously knew those in the upper echelons more intimately, I do not mean to imply otherwise; he knew their strengths, and ... far more to the point ... their weaknesses. But he also knew by sight, and in many cases by name, the most humble wretches who were working for him. In that knowledge was his strength, his power.' He lit another cigarette. 'Let us return, and see if Lefevre has anything to tell us.'

'By the way, Holmes,' said I innocently enough, 'you were wrong about one thing.'

'Indeed?'

'You thought that the assassination of the President was in some way linked to this gang ... now Jean-Paul tells us categorically that it was not!'

Holmes shook his head as if to dismiss this slur. 'Perhaps not directly,' said he. 'But it foreshadowed even worse things, did it not? It was the overall impression that I sensed. Perhaps I erred as to some minor details, but you must allow that I got all the important points correct.'

What could one do, faced with such monstrous egotism? I fairly gasped at this colossal perversion of the facts, and Holmes – thinking no doubt that I was lost in admiration of his brilliance – smiled complacently and set off along the street.

I noticed that on the way back to the *pension* Holmes kept a sharp look out, and I endeavoured to do the same, but I could not see anyone suspicious. Lefevre was waiting in our room once more, and Holmes told him in a very few words what we had been doing, adding finally, 'It might be as well if we did not meet for a while. We are almost certain to be watched carefully, although I am confident that we are safe for the moment.'

Lefevre nodded. 'Agreed. You can contact me via the owner here in an emergency, of course.'

'Did you manage to find anything about a "Monsieur Constantine", then?'

'There is a man of that name, in the right general locality.'

'Excellent!'

'But he is too old ... almost eighty. He is an importer of carpets.'

'Ah.'

'And there is his grandson.'

'But?'

'But he is too young,' said Lefevre with a smile. 'Only nineteen.'

'What about the son?' asked Holmes.

Lefevre shook his head. 'Dead, unfortunately. To be sure, there are half a dozen others, but they are all the wrong age, or living in the wrong locality, or there is some other obvious objection which rules them out.'

'He is, we know, the head of a private bank.'

Lefevre shrugged. 'There are many private banks in Paris ... always assuming that he told you the truth about that ... and I have checked as many as I could, but without success.'

'H'mm,' said Holmes. 'Well, it was worth a try. Constantine may be a Christian name, of course, or an alias. More likely the latter. In any event, that particular scent has gone cold, for the time being.'

'Do you have plans for today?' asked Lefevre. 'You have perhaps received some orders from the gang leaders?'

'Only to report at nine tomorrow, to see what duties may be required of us. I shall give you the address of the meeting place,' and Holmes scribbled it on a piece of paper.

'We shall keep an eye on it, you may be sure,' promised Lefevre.

'By the way,' said Holmes, 'speaking of keeping watch, you have not had us followed, have you?'

Lefevre looked puzzled, and shook his head. 'Not I.'

'H'mm. We were certainly followed from the *bistro*, and I thought I spotted someone even earlier, but I may have been mistaken there.'

'I had the same sensation!' said I.

'That is final, then. But it was not the police, you say?'

Lefevre shook his head again.

'It was most likely Jean-Paul's doing,' I said.

'This last time, perhaps,' said Holmes. 'But it was certainly very prescient of the gang to follow us earlier, before they even knew of our existence! There is something odd here ... unless both of us were mistaken. As for today,' he went on, 'I shall take a walk round the quarter. Watson here has already had the opportunity to acquaint himself with our surroundings, but I fear I have not, and ... although this area is not completely unfamiliar to me ... I do not know my way round as well as I might wish. I do not know if Watson would care to join me in my gentle stroll?'

'I had thought of going as far as the Place de l'Etoile,' said I, 'and see if I cannot spot our lodgings of the night before last.'

'Capital!' said Holmes.

'In that case,' said Lefevre, 'I shall wish you both *au revoir* and hope that you have good hunting!' He shook hands with us, and took his leave.

Holmes and I gave Lefevre a few minutes' grace, so that we did not seem too obviously connected with him, and then made our way downstairs and out into the street.

'I shall expect you at dinner time,' said Holmes, and, after tipping his hat to a jaunty angle, he sauntered off like any sightseer.

I set off in the opposite direction to that Holmes had taken. It was a beautiful day, I was not under any obligation to be at a specific place at a specific time – not until such time as I should meet Holmes that evening, anyway – and my ill-gotten gains nestled snugly in my pocket. I believe that I was as much at ease with the world as any man in Paris.

I made my way to the Rue Mouffetard, and there took a cab, asking the driver to take me to the Place de l'Etoile. The Place was crowded, as always, and as I stood on the pavement, irresolute, a sense of the futility of my task came upon me. What a fool I had been, to imagine for one moment that I could retrace a journey made in the dark, in a carriage whose blinds were drawn!

The crowds continued to push past me as I tried valiantly to consider the best thing to do. There are some seven or eight broad avenues leading from the Place – I have never bothered to count them exactly – but perhaps the two best-known to the English visitor are the Champs-Elysées, and the Avenue leading to the Bois. The Champs-Elysées looked particularly busy and dusty, as people sought their luncheon. But to my left it seemed quieter, the Bois lay at a distance of less than a mile, and there I could rest in the shade and the greenery. The choice was not a difficult one, after all, and I set off along the Avenue du Bois de Boulogne at a leisurely pace, staring about me as I went.

The shade here was pleasant, and there was certainly no shortage of imposing mansions; just the sort of place, thought I, in which Holmes and myself had been more or less uninvited guests. Who could say just what might go on behind these grand façades, these great doors and shuttered windows? Why – but my train of thought was interrupted, as I stumbled and bumped into a young lady. She had evidently been coming from one of those very mansions, perhaps to take luncheon with some fortunate young man; whilst I had been gawping like any day-tripper, instead of looking where I was going.

I hastily drew back, but the young lady had managed to drop her parasol in the confusion. Now, dear reader, I think I might make a guess as to what you are thinking, and if it had been London, or if the circumstances had been different, I cannot say but that your guess might be correct. But it was so palpably an accident; and the young woman was so clearly a lady, and so clearly belonged here, in these august surroundings; and then her expression showed a sort of pretty confusion, but no trace of coarseness, or of invitation; and so without hesitation I picked up her parasol, and handed it to her.

'A thousand pardons, Madame,' I told her.

'Mademoiselle,' said she, blushing delicately. 'Mademoiselle Marie Huret.'

Eight

Marie! For a moment, I was taken aback, for the name was so much like that of my wonderful, departed wife. And then this young lady was so much like Mary in appearance, blonde, with a most striking face – not at all the conventional 'beauty' such as may be seen in the society pages of any illustrated weekly paper, but with a delicacy and refinement which gave promise of a most wondrous character. All this conspired to deprive me of the power of thought for a moment; I stood there blushing and speechless, like any schoolboy at his first dance, until at long last I managed to stammer out, 'Er ... Harris. Harry Harris.'

''Arry 'Arris?' said she in English, with a most charming accent. 'Then you are surely an Englishman? I knew it! I knew it at once, when you bumped into me just now ... I could tell by your so charming accent that you were no true Frenchman!'

Damnation, I thought! What would Holmes say? What should he say – what, indeed, could he say, other than most strident and well-deserved words of reproof and objurgation? I could almost hear that cynical voice in my ear now – 'Watson, Watson! Ever the same old Watson! The merest glimpse of a pretty face, and all our careful work is undone in an instant! You did try to confuse her, of course, by using my alias instead of your own! But then on the debit side, you managed to tell her your middle name ... something that took me ten years to discover ... in the first two minutes of your acquaintance! Well done, old chap! It is good to have someone who may be relied upon to be remain a fixed point in an ever-changing age!'

Come, come now, Holmes, I told the stern critic seated on my shoulder – it is not quite that bad. True, I may have forgotten for the moment that I am currently passing myself off as Monsieur Henri Vert; and perhaps I also inadvertently omitted to recall that Henri should really be rendered in English as 'Mr Price.' But then this cloak-and-dagger business has never been a strong point with me; I know it is the very breath of life to you, Holmes, just as it was with that strange species, the Indian Political Officers, who were forever blacking themselves up and dressing in native costume – aye, and using names that were not their own! I was always more a man of action, one for acting in the open, and by the light of day, rather than concealing my true nature under any disguise. But for all that, this lady does not know my real name – and what matter if she did? How could that affect the outcome of our adventures? Answer me that, Holmes!

I became painfully aware that the young lady was looking intently at me, as if she expected some reply.

'Ah, yes,' I managed. 'That is, you are absolutely right ... I am, indeed, English. From ... ah, Portsmouth, you know.'

'I do not know it,' said she. 'But doubtless Monsieur also has the opportunity to visit London frequently ... with his wife, perhaps?'

'My wife, alas, is dead,' said I, 'some two or three years ago.'

'Oh! But I am so sorry to hear it! Monsieur, then is obliged to visit London alone; that is so sad! But then it must always cheer him up to see so beautiful, so wonderful a city ... I have never been to London, though I have always wanted to go there. It must be such fun to see the *boutiques*, the *grands magasins* ... and, of course, the famous places. Oxford Street, with its shops; Regent Street; Baker Street. Monsieur will know all these famous places so well, *n'est-ce pas?*

'Well, er ... that is, I have been there once or twice, of course. As, indeed, most people have. Well, I am sorry to have collided with you in such an uncivil fashion, but it has been a delight talking to you, Mademoiselle. There seems no real harm done, and so ...'

'Oh' she cried suddenly, taking hold of my arm, 'I am so sorry, Monsieur, but I feel a little faint.'

'It is the shock,' said I. 'You had best go and sit down for a moment. Is this your house?' and I pointed back to the great mansion from which I took it that she had just emerged.

'Yes. But I am not ill, merely shaken. There is no need to go back home and worry Monsieur Huret ... my uncle, of course ... he is a very busy man, and has many cares already. Perhaps Monsieur would be so kind as to take me to the café on the corner, there, and sit with me whilst I have a cup of tea?'

'Of course! Tea would be the finest thing for you! Settle your nerves at once!'

'I have the English taste, you see!' she said, smiling at me.

We set off for the little café which stood at no great distance.

'But tell me,' said Mademoiselle Huret, 'Monsieur is surely a doctor, that he diagnoses so quickly what is wrong?'

Watson! Watson! The words rang in my ear, so clearly that I turned round, fully expecting to find Holmes there!

'No, no. Not at all,' I mumbled, as we reached the café. 'Just a lucky guess, that was all.'

'I think Monsieur is being modest.'

We sat down, and I ordered some tea. 'Would you care for something to eat?' I asked. 'I was just going to have lunch myself, as a matter of fact.'

'No, thank you. Well, perhaps just a little something, then.'

We ate, and talked. Mademoiselle Huret asked me all manner of questions about myself, about England in general, and London in particular. And I endeavoured to answer as best I could, but always maintaining my role as a provincial visitor.

When the meal was over – all too quickly, as far as I was concerned! – I took Mademoiselle back to her grand house, and left her at the gate. There was no suggestion that I should do otherwise, and I did not expect any. In the hour or so we had spent together, there had been not the slightest hint of any sort of romantic dalliance; Mademoiselle was so much younger than I, for one thing, and so much like my own dear wife. Indeed, were it not too fanciful – or, the cynical reader will perhaps say, too precious – I should have said that Mademoiselle Huret put me in mind of the daughter whom I might have had, if circumstances had been somewhat different. To have presumed in any way upon our acquaintance would have been unthinkable.

As we said goodbye, though, she stood on her toes, and kissed me on the cheek. And then she was gone, with me staring after her like a schoolboy.

The last couple of hours had cheered me up considerably, and I resolved to continue with my search for Constantine's house. I set off, therefore, towards the Bois, looking left and right as I went. After no more than ten minutes, though, my new-found mood of optimism had evaporated. What on earth was I thinking about, to suppose that I was, in some mysterious fashion, likely to stumble upon one mansion, the right mansion, amongst so many? Why, I was not even sure that I was heading in the right direction, much less that I was in the right thoroughfare!

Then I thought again of Mademoiselle Huret, and I could not be too angry with myself. Instead, I laughed aloud at my foolishness, thereby startling a tall, distinguished and well-dressed gentleman who happened to be passing. He was in the company of a very young and very flamboyant lady, who was not, I think, his wife; and I rather suspect that he thought that I was passing some comment on his conduct. I mumbled 'Pardon,' but I do not think it helped.

I walked on, and then, struck by something about the appearance of the couple I had just bumped into, I turned to look back. There was no sign of them, which was odd, as there was no side road. They must, of course, have gone into one of the great houses that lined the road, I told myself. For all that, there was something odd – something familiar, I should have said – about the man's appearance. Where had I seen him before? I thought for a moment, then gave it up and went on my way.

I may have been more cheerful, but I was no more optimistic than I had been a moment or two before. To approach the job of finding Constantine's house as if it were a job that I could reasonably hope to do, a goal that might be achieved, was clearly preposterous – if Fate wanted me to find the place, then she would lead me there!

Rather than waste more time, then, on a fruitless task, I did as I had originally intended, and went as far as the Bois, where I spent the next two or three hours in quiet contemplation. So quiet and so contemplative was I, in fact, that I woke with a start to find, after consulting my watch, that I would have to hurry if I wanted to get back and meet Holmes in time for dinner.

Holmes had already returned to the *pension* when I arrived, and I could see at once that he looked somewhat on edge.

'Not late, am I?' I asked.

'Not at all, Doctor.'

'Good!' said I, with a sigh of relief. 'What a glorious day, Holmes! I have really enjoyed myself today!'

He leaned over, and took from my lapel – a single, blonde hair! 'So I observe,' said he.

'Nonsense, Holmes! Nothing of that sort, I assure you!'

'I am delighted to hear it.'

Wishing to change the subject, I asked him, 'I trust you have had an enjoyable stroll ... although I rather suspect otherwise.'

Holmes laughed. 'I never was very good at concealing my impatience,' said he. 'But it is not your lateness that makes me restless, nor yet an unseemly eagerness for my dinner. It is the fact that we must wait until tomorrow for a chance at the gang ... and even then, we may be told merely that we are not wanted for work today, for all the world like some poor longshoreman at the dock gates.'

'Oh, it may not be so bad ... we did promise ourselves a week or so before we tried another approach, did we not?'

'You are right, of course,' said he.

'Well, then ... how did you pass your day?' I enquired.

'Pretty much as I had intended ... I have been sauntering round the immediate environs, both to fix the geography in my mind and to gauge, so far as might be possible, the disposition of the local inhabitants.'

'And did you succeed?'

'I did with the former. The latter ... well, it is a curious thing, Watson, but ... tell me, how would you describe our surroundings?'

'Squalid,' said I bluntly. 'Doubtless it was once a patrician neighbourhood, but the centuries have not been as kind as they might.'

'Exactly! It is run-down, dirty. Very much like the East End of London, in fact, but with little of the camaraderie and good humour ... even if of a rough, gallows type ... that exists among our cockneys.'

'That is pretty much my own conclusion,' said I, puzzled to know what he was driving at.

'That being the case, you would expect a good deal of petty lawlessness, would you not? And yet on my ramble I saw no great evidence of anything untoward. It is true that I had one or two offers from such of the ladies of the town as had managed to be up and about relatively early, but there were no brawls in the markets, no cries of "Stop thief!" in the streets and alleys. Old ladies held their purses out in plain view, unafraid of pickpockets. What say you to that?'

'Well, that is surely no bad thing!' said I with a laugh. 'Say, though ... are you suggesting that there was no petty crime because all the local criminals have been recruited into this gang, and are waiting for bigger things?'

Holmes nodded. 'That is precisely what I am saying.'

'I see! Of course, from the point of view of the old ladies, and what have you, it is no detriment.'

'Of course not.'

'But standing back to look at the whole canvas ...'

'Ah, that is a different picture, is it not?'

'It is indeed,' said I. 'For it implies that some larger villainy is in prospect.'

'My conclusion exactly.'

'It is rather a pity that we cannot predict exactly what it might be, Holmes!'

'Now, that is true to some extent. We cannot, as you say, predict just when the next attempt on a bank or a post office will be, let us say. But we can perhaps look beyond that, and see what Jean-Paul's mysterious "chief" may have in mind for the longer term.'

'I scarcely follow you there, I fear.'

'Well, you heard Jean-Paul say that "the chief" was angry that the President had been assassinated.'

'Yes, indeed.' I hesitated. 'And ...'

Holmes sighed. 'And why should Bill Sykes, a common crook, mind who sits in the Presidential Palace? One head of state is surely much like another, to the average blackguard.'

'I see! Yes, Jean-Paul did say that some silly so-and-so had "jumped the gun", or something to that effect, did he not? And he drew parallels between this "chief" and Napoleon, which I rather suspected were somewhat exaggerated. But now it looks as if he may have read the situation quite correctly. In a sense, then, the assassination of the President ... tragedy though it is, heinous though it is ... may have prevented a yet greater tragedy.'

He shrugged. 'Perhaps.'

'But, Holmes! That makes no sense! You heard Jean-Paul ... even if he were not exaggerating, and this "chief" really does plan some kind of *coup d'état* ... the whole apparatus which would have enabled him to take power was not in readiness.'

'True. But you do not imagine that would stop a determined man?'

'But my point is that it did stop him! There has been no *coup*, Holmes!'

'Ah, not this time.'

'But ...' I stopped, and stared at him. 'Do you mean that once the apparatus *is* in place ...'

Holmes nodded calmly.

'Then,' said I, my head spinning, 'the next President is ... will be ...'

'Very far from safe. Just so, Doctor. Hence my impatience, for I have no doubt that this "chief" will be accelerating his plans now.'

'And why is that?'

'Because the assassination will have provoked some hard thinking amongst the forces of law and order no less than amongst the forces of evil. It may well be that the next President will not make quite so many public appearances. Or that the presidential bodyguard will be increased in numbers. Or that there will be a general round-up of anarchists and known or suspected criminals ... as I told you, Dubuque and Lefevre were planning to move against "our" anarchist ring before ever you and I came to Paris. The man we seek will have worked all that out; he will want to move quickly, before all these measures can be put into force and make his task more difficult, if not downright impossible.'

'I see! You are right, of course. I understand your impatience, now.'

'Let us hope that we make some progress soon,' said Holmes. He stood up. 'If you are ready to dine, Doctor, so am I.'

I fear that my appetite was not as hearty that evening as is my wont; while Holmes ate practically nothing. I did not, as I have on so many occasions, remonstrate with him over this fact, for I knew that he was thinking, trying to produce a plan of campaign which did not depend on mere blind Fate.

And for all that it was Fate which moved our investigation along, as you shall see. I was a long time getting off to sleep that night, for I was thinking over what Holmes had said, and trying in my own small way to see whether I might provide any suggestions which might contribute something to his eventual strategy.

I woke to find Holmes dressed and shaved. 'Are you ready for breakfast?' he asked me. 'I confess I am somewhat sharp-set, as the falconers say.'

'Your own fault, Holmes!' I told him, getting out of bed. 'You should have eaten properly last night.'

'Ah, but I was thinking,' said he.

'And have you reached any conclusion?'

'Only that I shall have a decent breakfast!' he answered. 'And then we shall see if we are needed today. If not, then we shall try to find another scent, and work that independently of Jean-Paul and his little band. What say you to that, Doctor?'

'Capital! The thought of inaction is anathema to me.' And, that now being settled, I made every bit as hearty a breakfast as did Holmes.

We walked to the little *bistro* as we had been ordered, arriving there at ten minutes before nine. The back room was already crowded, there being perhaps twice as many people in there as we had seen the day before, and this time there were women among them. My first thought was that Holmes's deductions were proved appallingly correct, and that there was some grand enterprise planned for that very day. In the event I was wrong; and I subsequently concluded that on the previous day we had arrived there somewhat later than nine o'clock, with the result that some of the gang had already left on their various enterprises.

We got some curious looks from those who had not seen us the previous day, and one or two of them came forward rather shyly to introduce themselves. There was 'Maurice the Knife,' I recall, a likeable enough fellow with a Northern accent you could cut with what I assume was his favourite weapon; and 'Denis the Dip,' and 'Fifi the Hell-cat,' and one or two others I cannot bring to mind. These civilities were interrupted by the arrival of Jean-Paul, who gave out his orders with the minimum of formality. Some were told to go to a certain place, or to report to a certain person; some were told merely, 'As previously agreed,' and these would nod and leave; and finally, some poor souls were told, 'Nothing for you today.' These latter seemed genuinely upset that they had not been deemed worthy, and I could almost find it in me to feel sorry for them.

Holmes and I were left until the very last, so that it was only when the room was empty apart from the three of us that Jean-Paul finally said, with a touch of wonder in his voice, 'Well, my lads! Ready for something a little special, are you?'

'Indeed, yes!' said I, while Holmes nodded.

'That's good! And it's a great compliment, I can tell you, to be selected so soon in your careers for something this big! Now then, someone wants a word with you.' Jean-Paul went over to a door in the far corner of the room, and tapped on it.

The door opened, and out came our old friend, Monsieur Constantine. He bowed to us. 'I hoped that we should perhaps meet again,' he told us.

'You have a job for us?' asked Holmes.

'Perhaps.' From under his cloak, Constantine took a magazine.

My heart sank! I recognized the front cover of the *Strand*, indeed the very volume which contained my very first short story about Holmes, 'A Scandal in Bohemia.' How often had I glanced proudly at that magazine, or left it lying casually about where my friends might notice it! I silently cursed the fact that I was unarmed. True, my revolver was in my pocket – but I had foolishly omitted to load it!

'You have, perhaps, seen this before?' Constantine was asking us, waving the magazine.

With an effort, I told him, 'No, not I.'

Holmes shook his head. 'Nor I.'

Constantine spread the magazine on the table, and flicked over its pages. 'Ah, yes.'

I saw to my horror that he had turned to my own story of the King of Bohemia and Miss Irene Adler!

'What say you to that?' asked Constantine.

Holmes looked over his shoulder. 'I can make out only a few words of English,' said he, 'but it seems to me to be singularly wanting in literary skill.'

'Nonsense!' said I. 'Why, even if one knows no English at all, one must admire the simple, strong, short sentences, and the elegant way in which the paragraphs ...'

'This is not a literary circle, *mes amis*!' cried Constantine. 'It is *that* upon which I want your opinion!' and he stabbed with a finger at the page.

I looked where he indicated, and if my heart had sunk earlier, it positively missed a beat – or two – now. Constantine's finger was tapping against one of the illustrations. An illustration which showed me sitting at my ease in an armchair before the fire at 221B Baker Street; while Mr Sherlock Holmes stood leaning against the mantelpiece talking to me!

Nine

'Well? And what of it?' said Holmes in the most off-hand manner you could imagine.

'This fellow standing warming his backside at the fire,' said Constantine. 'Do you not think he resembles you, more or less?'

Holmes picked up the *Strand*, and made a great show of studying the illustration. 'I can see no similarity, to speak plainly,' he said, with as much indifference as before, tossing the magazine back to Constantine.

'And you, Monsieur Vert?' Constantine handed the magazine across to me.

I glanced at it. 'Not the slightest resemblance,' said I, and meant it.

I could see that Constantine was puzzled by my stout denial. As I read it, Constantine had seen the *Strand* illustration – heaven knows how, unless perhaps one of his men had drawn his attention to it – and he entertained some suspicions of Holmes. But he was not absolutely sure of the identification, and meant to test Holmes and myself, to see what our reaction might be. According to that reaction, Constantine would judge us guilty or innocent.

Now, Holmes can always be relied upon to give nothing away unless he really wants to; he possesses the most immobile countenance of any man I have met, when he chooses. And then my own rejection of Constantine's suggestion sounded authentic, for the simple reason that it was authentic – there was, in very truth, not the least resemblance between Holmes and the supposed representation of him as shown in the *Strand* illustration, and for an excellent reason, which may already be known to some of my readers.

When the owners of the *Strand* saw fit to publish my own efforts, they sought to commission Walter Paget, a rising young artist, to provide the illustrations. Now, Walter had a brother, Sidney, who was also an artist, and by some curious mischance, the *Strand* owners asked Sidney, and not Walter, to provide the drawings. Sidney had never met Holmes, he had merely read my own descriptions, imperfect though these may have been; and Sidney therefore chose his brother Walter as the model for the drawings!

Fear not, dear reader; there is a point, a moral almost, to this somewhat lengthy tale, for Walter was a man of striking good looks. He might have made a living on the stage as a juvenile lead with no difficulty; and this showed in Sidney's illustrations. By contrast, Holmes – though possessed of no end of sterling qualities – was totally devoid of any favourable traits of physiognomy. His face was striking, indeed; but his best friends and staunchest admirers could never in this world call him handsome.

For my part, I had nothing to fear. Sidney had drawn me as something of a foppish man about town, although he had perhaps not taken quite so many liberties with my appearance as he had with Holmes's – indeed, I like to think that there was less need for flattery in my case – and thus any resemblance between me and Sidney's representation of me in the *Strand*, particularly as I had put on a few pounds in weight over the last four or five years, was of the flimsiest.

Constantine, as I say, was clearly at something of a loss. He had perhaps expected Holmes and me to bluster, or to run, or to admit the deception – at any event, to do something that would prove his suspicions correct; and so Holmes's calm indifference and my blunt denial threw him somewhat. He handed the *Strand* to Jean-Paul. 'Let us have your opinion.'

Jean-Paul shook his head. 'This Englishman in the magazine is an *aristo*, that's clear enough. Good-looking, too! While Pierre here ... well, no offence, *mon vieux*, but ... no, not the least alike. Both tall, of course,' he added, as if trying to salvage something for Constantine.

'Very well, then. And now, if you will, your opinion on this, Messieurs.' Constantine took a small photograph from his pocket, and laid it carefully down before us.

I have said that I had recovered my wits by now, and it was just as well, for the photograph was of Holmes himself, wearing a frock coat and top hat, outside the door of 221B Baker Street! Fortunately, I myself did not appear in the picture, or I cannot say what I might have said or done.

'Well?' Constantine asked me.

'Well ... perhaps in this instance ... yes, one might possibly think that there is some passing resemblance to this fellow,' was the best that I could manage – I could not in all conscience try to deny it, for the likeness was plain to see, despite the fact that the photograph had evidently been taken hastily and by an amateur.

'Jean-Paul?'

'This one is closer than the magazine picture, to be sure.' He regarded Holmes critically. 'If you would turn your head, Pierre ... so! Well, when the light falls thus ... yes! He might pass for the man in the photograph.'

Holmes took the photograph, and pretended to study it. 'He is not so tall,' he pointed out. 'Nor by any means as good-looking!'

'Yes, but could you impersonate him?' asked Constantine.

Holmes strolled over to a blotchy mirror, on which a scantily clad lady advertised the supposed virtues of a once-popular brand of *absinthe*. He held his head on one side, and studied the photograph again. 'The clothes, the hat ... what of them?'

'Well, but there are tailors, hatters, what you will!' said Constantine.

'You would really wish me to impersonate this fellow?'

'It would be of the greatest help to us.'

'In that case ... I will do it!'

'Very well.' Constantine took the photograph from Holmes and looked at it again. 'You had best go to the tailor's right away. Jean-Paul here will provide you with the necessary funds for a new outfit.'

'And what is it you wish me to do, may one ask?'

'All in good time,' said Constantine. 'Be ready by noon today.'

'It ... whatever it may be ... is planned for today, then?'

Constantine nodded. 'This afternoon! Jean-Paul will explain nearer the time; and I shall see you when the task is completed.' He bowed, and was gone almost before we had realized it.

'You've certainly made an impression!' said Jean-Paul admiringly. He unlocked a cupboard and produced a small cash box, from which he took a sheaf of notes. 'If there's any change, so much the better!' he told Holmes. 'And ... change or no change ... I want receipts for everything you buy, or it'll come out of your cut!'

Holmes and I set off down the alley. 'A pity we were not told the details!' said I. 'Or we might have informed Dubuque.'

'I am certain the omission was intentional. These fellows take no chances, even with those whom they believe can be trusted. We are, as you have no doubt noticed, being followed now.'

'What?'

'Keep your voice down!' hissed Holmes. 'Yes, there are two of them ... one this side, twenty feet behind us, and one on the other side of the road.'

'Suspicious dogs! Well, that rules out our telling Dubuque anything ... even if we actually knew anything!'

'In any event,' said Holmes, 'I am not sure I should have informed Dubuque after all ... we may be better advised to play a lone hand, and see how things turn out.'

'When was that photograph taken, think you?'

'I wondered that myself. Probably after your marriage, I should think, for you were not in the photograph. Were I pressed for an answer, I should say that it was late in the 'eighties, when I began the Moriarty investigation in earnest. I have no recollection of being asked to smile for the camera, so

102

I take it that it was concealed ... one of these vest pocket devices, hidden in a cigarette case or a watch, at a guess. It is perhaps as well, for a better photograph would have given the game away at once!'

'Perhaps it was taken by one of Moriarty's agents, Holmes?'

'Almost certainly it was taken by one of his agents, Watson. Moriarty left nothing to chance.'

'And now Moriarty returns, as it were, to haunt you!'

'Indeed.'

'It is certainly ironic that they should ask you to impersonate yourself!'

Holmes looked thoughtful. 'I trust it *is* merely one of life's little ironies, Watson, and not something more sinister. I confess that it took all the self-control of which I was capable, back there.'

'Lord, yes! I was never more frightened in my life! I thought we were discovered, and expected to feel a knife in my ribs at any moment!'

'You handled it very well, I must say. Your stubborn refusal to see what was in front of you ...'

'A trait honed by years of practice, according to you, Holmes!'

'Well, if I have slighted you once or twice in the past in that respect, then at any rate I give you my unstinting praise now, Doctor! Your persistence bought me time to arrange my own scattered thoughts.' He lapsed into silence for a moment. 'For all that it seems to have passed off rather well, I cannot pretend that I am entirely happy. We may perhaps not have been completely unmasked, but, once the resemblance has been noticed ...' and he shook his head. 'I really think, Watson, that I shall have to forbid any further publication of my adventures, for the time being at least. This publicity is not merely inconvenient, it is becoming positively dangerous! When once I am retired, of course ...'

'We can perhaps discuss that later, Holmes,' said I. Keen to change the subject, I went on, 'Did you not tell me back in London that this mysterious head of the gang, the "chief" of whom Jean-Paul spoke, did you not say that he himself had impersonated you on an earlier occasion?'

'I did.'

'Then why,' I wanted to know, 'does he not do so now?'

Holmes laughed. 'That, at least, is explicable,' said he. 'On that first occasion, there was nobody else who looked like me. He was obliged, therefore, to take the very considerable risk of appearing in person. But now ... well, one does not keep a dog and bark oneself! If he can achieve the same result, but let me ... or Pierre Leblanc, rather ... take all the risks, so much the better, from his point of view.'

'This development might be of the greatest use to us, Holmes?'

'Just so, Doctor.' He grew serious. 'But nevertheless, we must go carefully here, Watson ... we must go very carefully indeed!'

There was insufficient time to visit a tailor's and get anything made to measure, so we settled for a men's outfitters in the middle range, where Holmes was soon provided with a respectable enough morning coat and a top hat. 'You look quite your old self!' I told him, as he regarded himself critically in the shopman's glass.

'That is what bothers me!' he answered, and repeated, 'We must go very carefully now!'

We set off back, and I fancied that I saw one at least of the men who were following us; but the second had evidently left us, unless he were very well hidden. At the *bistro*, Jean-Paul regarded Holmes with some approval. 'Quite the gent, aren't we?' he said. 'Now, a spot of luncheon ... nothing to drink, mind! We need clear heads for the afternoon's work.' He led the way to what I might term the legitimate section of the *bistro*, and ordered something or the other for all three of us.

I confess that I did not even notice what was on the plate before me, much less did I eat any of it – not because it was in any way unappetizing, but the thought of what was to come blunted any appetite I might otherwise have had. I noticed that Holmes, too, merely picked at his food.

Jean-Paul seemed to find our reluctance to eat amusing. 'Nerves, it it?' he asked, in his blunt fashion. 'Well, that may be all to the good ... keep you alert, and so forth.' He himself did not seem to be at all dissuaded from eating, and in fact he selected a few choicer items from my plate, and Holmes's too. When he had done, he looked at us with some concern. 'Not too nervous, are you? I mean, if it bothers you, we can call it off ...'

'Not at all!' said Holmes, adding carelessly, 'I never eat before a big job ... ask Henri here if you doubt it.'

'True enough,' said I. 'I have often protested about it, but to no avail. Although I must admit that my own appetite is not usually so poor. Excitement at being selected so early in our career, I suppose.'

'Yes, indeed,' said Jean-Paul. 'It's quite an honour, I can tell you! The other lads will be jealous as hell!'

'We do not yet know the full details of your plan,' said Holmes.

'No.' Jean-Paul, who had been speaking in his usual tones, evidently feeling safe enough in these familiar surroundings, now looked round and lowered his voice. 'Diamonds!'

'Diamonds?'

'Keep your voice down! Yes, a jeweller's in the Rue de la Paix, near the Place Vendôme.'

'Very exclusive, no doubt?' said Holmes.

'Not half! Very classy, very snob. Anyway, he's had a delivery of diamonds just lately, from Antwerp.' Jean-Paul produced a grimy bit of paper from his pocket. 'That's the name of the cutter, and what have you ... you'll read it quicker than I, one has no doubt. Now, what do you think that gent is, the one in the photograph, the one you're supposed to be?'

Holmes shrugged his shoulders. 'Well? What is he, then?'

'A detective!'

'What!'

'Yes,' said Jean-Paul. 'An English detective, very famous ... none other than the famous Sherlock Holmes!' He laughed until he almost choked, and I slapped him on the back. 'Thanks, Henri. Yes, my lads! What do you think to that for cheek?'

'And I am to impersonate this ... this Shylock Holmes?'

'Sherlock. Yes, indeed.' Jean-Paul reached into his greasy coat again, and carefully took out a crisp white visiting card. I looked at it with some interest, and saw that it was one of Holmes's own – easy enough to acquire, in all conscience, for a man hands out dozens of the things without thinking, and does not, as a rule, demand their return. I have no doubt that Moriarty, or one of his lieutenants, had obtained the card several years before, and preserved it meticulously ever since, lest it might prove useful. That one fact alone told me a great deal about the organization we were fighting.

'Now,' Jean-Paul was telling Holmes, 'you're to go to this shop ... I'll take you there ... and spin them some yarn or the other. Identify yourself ... show them your visiting card ... and tell them, oh, that there's been a tip-off, a gang of crooks is after the stones. Mention the names on that scrap of paper, talk as if you knew all about the shipment, and point out that what you know, thieves can know too. Ask to see the diamonds, to check they're safe, that sort of thing.'

'Perhaps he might hint that the stones have already been replaced by fakes?' I suggested.

'Capital!' said Jean-Paul. 'I knew you were the right lads! Now, however you do it, you grab the sparklers, right? Then leg it, as fast as you can.'

'The jeweller will immediately call the police!' Holmes objected.

'Too true! There'll be a couple of *gendarmes* standing right outside the shop! And they will, naturally, give chase at once, and catch you right away! Only ...' and he broke off and laughed heartily – 'they'll be our lads, dressed up! They bundle you into a waiting cab, tell the jeweller that all's well, and he'll soon have his stones back ... and there you are! What say you to that?'

'Not half bad!' admitted Holmes. 'Simple,' he added thoughtfully, 'but perhaps more likely to work than a more elaborate plan, which would entail more that might go wrong.'

'Ah, that's the chief for you!' said Jean-Paul, every bit as delighted as if he had thought of it himself. 'None of your complicated ploys, where a man must be constantly troubling himself to remember details, but ... my word! They get the goods, I can tell you!'

'But what if the jeweller insists on going along with them?' I wanted to know. 'To keep an eye on his property.'

'*Merde!* More fool him, in that case!' said Jean-Paul, somewhat embarrassed. 'We won't hurt him, though ... just a tap on the head, and out he goes into the gutter, eh?' He wiped his chin, which gave some hint of his erstwhile meal, and stood up. 'Ready, then?'

'Ready,' said Holmes.

Jean-Paul had a cab standing in the road – I suspected then, and still suspect to this day, that the driver was in the employ of the gang, and did not ply for legitimate hire at all – and we soon crossed to the Right Bank, and headed briskly towards the Tuileries.

Jean-Paul nodded through the window. 'There's our lads.'

I followed his gaze, and saw two *gendarmes* standing at the corner. One raised his hand in a salute as the cab drew up, to show that all was well.

Jean-Paul nodded to Holmes. 'Up to you, now, Pierre,' he said. 'Good luck!' he added, as Holmes descended into the street.

I made as if to follow, but Jean-Paul's huge arm prevented me. 'Just watch the show,' he advised me. 'We'll have our bit of excitement soon enough, you'll see!'

I sat back, and watched through the cab window as Holmes entered the shop, and approached an assistant. There was a short exchange, then the assistant left Holmes staring at a display case. A moment later the assistant returned, accompanied by a short, stout man with a heavy black beard.

'The owner!' Jean-Paul hissed in my ear.

The owner, for such it was, listened as Holmes spoke long and earnestly. Then the owner seemed disposed to argue with Holmes, who produced the visiting card, and pointed to it.

'Clever!' said Jean-Paul.

The jeweller vanished, returning a moment later with a jewel case. He opened this, and indicated its contents, speaking volubly to Holmes as he did so. Holmes shrugged, and turned as if to leave in disgust. The jeweller stopped him, handed the case over. Holmes examined the stones, pointed and said something. It was now the jeweller's turn to shrug, as if he could not believe what Holmes was saying.

Then suddenly Holmes closed the case, pushed the jeweller out of the way, raced past the astonished assistant, and out into the street! The jeweller stumbled, bumped into the unfortunate assistant, swore at him – it was as well we could not lip-read, I fancy – and chased after Holmes.

Holmes, meantime, had dashed into the street, then stopped, uncertain, as if he had just noticed the *gendarmes* lounging there. The jeweller was not long following Holmes outside, and began to shout and wave his arms. Holmes now cast caution to the winds, and started to run down the street. The *gendarmes* followed at once, and Jean-Paul roared with laughter. 'Not half bad!' said he. 'Now, they'll ... *merde!*'

I followed his gaze, and was astonished to see a third *gendarme*, and then a fourth, emerge from a doorway, and block Holmes's flight! Holmes made as if to avoid them, but he was quickly seized. The first two *gendarmes* who had been chasing him stopped in their tracks, as if unsure what to do next.

'*Merde!*' repeated Jean-Paul.

'Not part of the plan?' I asked.

'*Merde, non!* Those are *real* policemen! What the devil are we to do now, Henri?'

I thought fast. I knew, of course – as Jean-Paul did not know – that Holmes had nothing to fear from the police. Dubuque would quickly sort out any silly misunderstanding. But there was a danger inasmuch as, having once been arrested Holmes could hardly reappear as if nothing had happened! This would spoil our chances of making ourselves useful to the gang, and to its mysterious chief.

The two fake *gendarmes* had now recovered their wits sufficiently to make as if to assist the real policemen, who were bundling Holmes into a cab. But even from where we sat it was obvious that the real policemen were politely but firmly declining the offer of assistance – and Jean-Paul's 'lads' clearly did not wish to press the matter.

The jeweller, all out of breath and flushed with anger, had now reached the little group, and began to protest volubly. One of the real *gendarmes* said something in a lofty fashion, then shrugged his shoulders. Meantime, his colleague urged Holmes into the cab with the toe of his boot.

'Just as in our plan!' said Jean-Paul sadly. 'They will have told the jeweller to go to the Palais de Justice, there to receive a receipt for the stones. *Merde!*' he mumbled, as the cab moved off. 'Any ideas, Henri?'

'We can follow them,' said I. 'Call your men in, and let's be off before we lose them.'

'Follow them? But why? Once at the Palais de Justice ...' and a great shrug ended the sentence.

'I have no idea what we can do,' said I, 'but we may think of something. Certainly, if we stay here, we shall never retrieve anything from this affair!'

'You're right.' Jean-Paul leaned out of the window, and whistled at his lads, who ran over and joined us. Jean-Paul shouted an order at the cabbie, and we moved off.

The two fake *gendarmes* looked unhappily at Jean-Paul. 'Nothing we could do, boss!' said one of them.

'No, no. I can't blame you.' Jean-Paul leaned out of the window again. 'Keep up, there!' he told the cabbie. 'Next turning left, they took.' He looked ruefully at me. 'Any inspiration yet?'

'Well ... when we reach the police station, why don't you and I start a fight. The real *gendarmes* will try to separate us ... they may even think that it's some scheme to rescue Pierre! ... and then these two can offer to guard Pierre whilst those two are busy with us.'

'H'mm.'

'Not much, I know, but that's the best I can think of at the moment.'

'It could work, you know. If we make it look convincing. Yes. It might work ... anyway, we've nothing else, so let's try that. Keep up, damn you!' he added to the cabbie.

'But which way, boss? We seem to have lost them.' The cab slowed down as he said the words.

'Damnation!' Jean-Paul leaped down into the road and stared about him. 'Which way *have* the dogs taken? Anybody see them?'

One of the fake *gendarmes* mumbled something.

'What d'you say?'

'This isn't the way to the Palais de Justice, you know! There's something wrong here, boss.'

'I think you're right,' said Jean-Paul. 'Look, you two go down there ...' he pointed, 'and Henri, come with me.'

We set off down a side street, and almost at once Jean-Paul pointed ahead. 'What's that? By the lamp post?'

'Good God!' said I. 'It's Hol ... it's old Pierre!'

It was indeed Holmes, slumped in the street! He had evidently been hit hard enough to stun him, but I could see no serious injury, and he groaned and tried to stand up as we reached him. Jean-Paul and I helped him to his feet.

He stared sorrowfully at us, then tried to laugh.

'What?' said Jean-Paul.

'It is really too funny!' Holmes was sufficiently recovered to laugh in his peculiar silent fashion.

'I can't see the joke, *mon ami!*'

'Jupin! That was Jupin, and one of his confederates!'

'What! Jupin? Then the diamonds ...'

'The diamonds are gone, I fear. Unless one could persuade Jupin to share them!'

Jean-Paul looked grim. 'The chief won't like this,' said he. 'Not one bit! You'll have to explain this to him in person, my lads!'

Holmes and I exchanged a glance, and I knew that we were both thinking the same thing. This turn of events meant that we should meet Jean-Paul's 'chief' at last – but the circumstances might have been slightly more favourable!

Jean-Paul's two *gendarmes* had reached us by now, and we returned, a gloomy little party, to the cab, and set off home.

'It was a curious coincidence, Jupin's being there!' I ventured.

'Coincidence be damned!' said Jean-Paul morosely. 'It is just the sort of theft that would appeal to him!'

'But, to use fake *gendarmes* ...'

'Now that *was* coincidence, I agree! But still ... great minds think alike!' And Jean-Paul lapsed into a brooding silence until we reached the little *bistro*.

Jean-Paul led the way inside, only to stop suddenly in the doorway of the usual back room. 'What the devil ... oh, sorry, Monsieur Constantine,' said he. 'I didn't see you there. And ... oh!' He nudged me violently in the ribs, and whispered, 'The chief!'

I followed him into the room, which held a half-dozen rough-looking men. I did not recognize any of them as being the men who had been there that morning, and

Jean-Paul was evidently at as much of a loss as I, for he asked, 'Who might these lads be, chief? And how did you know ...' and he stopped, and coughed, as if realizing that he had said too much already.

The man he had addressed was standing in a gloomy corner. He was a tall man, as tall as Holmes himself, and the lower part of his face was swathed in a white silk scarf. 'These are my own men,' said he, in a curious sibilant tone. He went on, 'And how did I know ... what?'

'Why ... the diamonds!'

'Ah, yes! The diamonds, to be sure! You have them?'

Jean-Paul shrugged. 'Alas, no! The plan went wrong! We thought they were real *gendarmes* ... they took Pierre ... but all the time it was Jupin!'

'Ah!' The mysterious 'chief' nodded his head. 'Jupin has the diamonds, then?'

'Of course!'

'Jupin! The mysterious, ubiquitous Jupin! Jupin, who may be relied upon to be always where he is needed, at the right time!'

'It *was* Jupin, chief!' Jean-Paul assured him.

'Of course! *Tant pis*, we shall discuss the diamonds later! But ... Jupin always excepted, of course ... the plan went well?'

'Well enough,' muttered Jean-Paul.

'Thank you, Jean-Paul, that will be all. I shall take over now. You can go.'

Jean-Paul looked rather askance at this, but he could not very well do anything other than leave, which he did with some evident reluctance.

I confess that I was now very worried. I have no doubt whatsoever that Jean-Paul was a rogue who would cut the throat of his proverbial grandmother for the equally proverbial couple of shillings, but by his own lights he was decent enough, and the fact that he had been sent out leaving us alone with these strangers seemed to me to bode no good.

'You had no difficulty impersonating Mr Sherlock Holmes?' said the man whose face we could not see.

'None whatsoever,' said Holmes calmly.

'No. But then, why should you? After all, there is no difficulty about impersonating oneself ... is there, Mr Sherlock Holmes!'

Holmes tensed himself to spring forward, but he was seized by two or three of the ruffians surrounding him. I, too, felt my arms grabbed from behind.

The mysterious 'chief' went on, 'I had you fooled from the start, Holmes! I recognized you at once, of course!'

'Of course, you did,' said Holmes calmly enough. 'I had hopes that you would! For how otherwise could I get to meet you so quickly?'

The other man seemed taken aback by this for a moment, then he said with a sneer, 'Sheer bluff, Holmes! Your plans have gone wrong ... why not simply admit as much?'

'Dubuque knows everything,' said Holmes as calmly as before.

'Dubuque? But ... ah, I see! Yes, that was clever. But, even though he is still alive, I rather fancy ...' and he looked at Constantine for confirmation.

Constantine shook his head. 'They have had no opportunity to tell Dubuque anything,' said he. 'Oh, the police watch this place ... we have known that all along ... but that is all, and the watchers are easily eluded. They have never yet spotted me, for instance!'

The 'chief' laughed. 'I thought as much!' To Holmes he said, 'You have spoiled my plans ... for I know this nonsense about Jupin is a lie! I should kill you now ... but I shall keep you alive ... for a time only, you understand, a very short time ... for I see another use for you yet.' He walked over, and studied me intently. 'However, I regret most deeply that I cannot say the same for you, Doctor Watson.' He stepped back, and nodded to the men who held my arms.

I felt a sudden, searing pain in my head, and then there was only blackness.

Ten

'Doctor Watson! Doctor Watson!'

I stirred, and groaned, conscious only of a terrible pain in my head. Then I believe I must have passed out again, and it seemed an age before I once again heard, 'Doctor Watson!'

I sensed, rather than saw, someone bending over me, and fearing that they intended me some further harm I struck out blindly and feebly. My arms were gripped, but not in any rough or unfriendly manner, and I finally recognized Dubuque's voice, although it was strained and anxious.

'Doctor Watson! Are you hurt?'

I opened my eyes, to shut them again quickly. 'Damned silly question, if ever I heard one!' I protested querulously.

'Ah, but then you cannot be too badly damaged!'

'No, I ... ouch!' I rubbed my head ruefully. 'No blood, though,' I added, looking at my hand. I glanced around. We were in a narrow court or alley, which I judged – correctly in the event – must be behind the *bistro*. From the light, I could tell that the evening was drawing in. 'What on earth is the time?' I asked Dubuque.

'Eight o'clock.'

'Good Lord! I must have been unconscious for some four or five hours, then! I say, Dubuque, how came you to find me here? I'm glad you did, of course, but how?'

'All in good time, *mon vieux*. I am still troubled as to whether or not you are badly injured.'

'Not a bit of it!'

Dubuque bent down and retrieved a battered object, which he handed to me. 'Your beautiful hat ... it is ruined, I think.'

'I think you are right,' said I. 'Poor old bowler! It evidently took the worst of the blow, and incidentally saved my life. I shall keep it as a souvenir, though I shall never dare sport it in Jermyn Street again.'

Dubuque dusted down my coat, which betrayed the fact that I had spent some time lying in the none too clean gutter. 'And you are well enough to travel?'

'Fine, fine!' I essayed a few steps, and stumbled against Dubuque. 'That is ... perhaps it might be as well if I were to sit down for a moment?'

Dubuque led me inside the little *bistro*, which was now quite deserted – oddly enough, considering the hour. I looked round, puzzled. 'Where is everyone, then? More to the point, Dubuque ... where is Holmes?'

'Ah, that I cannot say ... I had hopes that you might tell me, for it was partly Monsieur Holmes that I was seeking when I came here. Mostly, of course, I came to find you.'

'I see.' I confess that I did not; but I was having difficulty seeing anything for the moment, and did not feel inclined to engage in academic discussion. 'I wonder, Dubuque ... would there be a bottle of wine handy, think you?'

'We can, perhaps, do a little better than that,' and Dubuque passed me his silver flask.

'Cognac! Excellent!' I took a long pull, and handed the flask back to Dubuque, who regarded it with some sadness. 'Some people criticize me for prescribing brandy so freely, you know,' I told him.

'Ridiculous!'

'Absurd! I wonder ...'

'Of course!' He passed the flask back to me, and I drained it. 'I shall, of course, refill it for you at the earliest opportunity,' I assured him. 'Now, you were telling me that you came here looking for Holmes?'

'It is true.' Dubuque coughed, embarrassed. 'In connection with the jewel theft, you understand?'

'Jewel theft?' The blow on the head had caused me to forget the events of the day for a moment. 'Ah, yes. That can all be explained, of course. It was part of the plan.'

'Indeed?'

'Yes. Holmes will explain it all ...' then, as my head began to clear, I suddenly realized the significance of what Dubuque had said. 'Good Lord, Dubuque! Have you not found Holmes, then? And the villains?'

Dubuque shook his head. 'I shall explain. The jeweller in the Place Vendôme ... he found a *gendarme* ... a real *gendarme*, *bien entendu*, not a fake ... and made a complaint. Monsieur Holmes, he is identified ... why, he even left his card!'

'That can all be explained ...'

'Assuredly! But the examining magistrate ... you understand ... and then Monsieur Holmes was here under my aegis, so to speak, acting with my knowledge and my assistance, after all ... well, it is awkward, *mon ami*, there is no doubt of that. So, I look for Monsieur Holmes at the *pension*, but no, he is not there. Then I ask my man ... I have had a man watching this place, you understand ... and he says yes, Monsieur Holmes and the good Doctor, they have gone in, and not come out. But my man speaks also of a great crowd of men he cannot recognize ... they enter in the early afternoon, then Monsieur Holmes and Doctor Watson also enter, then the other men come out, very cheerful ...'

'Very cheerful?'

'Well, to speak plainly, a little drunk, you understand! Some are singing, some staggering ... one poor fellow has passed out, and the others are obliged to carry him!'

'The villains!' I cried. 'That was poor Holmes! They have drugged him, or knocked him unconscious, and that is how they got him out!'

'I did not know that, of course,' said Dubuque. 'But I knew that something must have gone horribly wrong. And then I received a note, delivered to my office.' He held a piece of paper out to me, and I read – 'If M. Dubuque wishes to speak to Dr Watson, he will find him in the alley behind a certain *bistro*.' There was no signature, merely the initials 'A J'.

'A J?' said I. 'Arsène Jupin!'

Dubuque nodded. 'That is what I tell myself! Jupin, then, is somehow involved in this affair! And so I come here and search the place, but we found nobody inside, apart from the owner and a couple of customers with little money and less gastronomic scholarship. Then I look out here ... and sure enough I find you! I tell you frankly, *mon ami*, that by now I have not the least idea as to what is going on! But at least I found you, and you are well! Well enough,' he amended.

'You say you found the proprietor and a couple of customers?'

'Nobody else was here. They are under arrest in the other room ... would you care to see them?'

I followed him next door, and took a good look at the men Dubuque had found; but I did not recognize either of the customers. The proprietor protested his innocence volubly, claiming that the hire of the back room was a business matter, nothing more or less, that he knew nothing of what went on in there, and so forth, and I was inclined to sympathize with his predicament. 'He is probably telling the truth,' I told Dubuque. 'Indubitably he knew they were rogues who had hired his room, but so long as they paid, and did not disturb the legitimate customers ...'

'Monsieur is absolutely correct!' the proprietor broke in eagerly.

'Very well,' said Dubuque. 'There will probably be no charges ... yet! But I think we shall keep you safe for the time being, all of you.'

And, despite some vigorous objections from the trio, they were duly taken off into police custody. 'It is as well,' Dubuque told me. 'They very likely are innocent, and know nothing of this gang, but on the other hand, there may be a spy among them, left to watch and report back what happens. We shall keep them until this affair is concluded. One way or the other,' he added rather gloomily.

'You do not sound overly optimistic,' said I.

Dubuque shrugged. 'What would you have me say? One must be realistic, Doctor, and the plain fact is that we still do not have a single clue.'

'What of Constantine?'

'That proved a dead end, did it not? I have no more information on this mysterious Constantine than I had earlier. But come, old friend ... you are still faint from the blow. We must see that you get a decent night's sleep, first of all.'

'But ... Holmes!' I protested.

'It will do Monsieur Holmes no good at all if Doctor Watson collapses and must go to the hospital, *n'est-ce pas?* No, a decent night's rest is what you need. We cannot take you back to the *pension*, for I am certain that they will be keeping watch there ... and besides, it is not a very nice place. No, you must come with me. I have an apartment ... only a bachelor's apartment, *bien entendu*, homely, Spartan even, but there is a spare room which has a comfortable bed, with silk sheets ...'

'Oh?'

'I told you,' said Dubuque carelessly, 'it is a bachelor's apartment.'

'Ah. Just so.'

I cannot remember just how I got to Dubuque's 'Spartan' apartment; the next thing I recollect is curling up in that comfortable bed between those silk sheets. I cannot say if it was the blow on the head, or the brandy, or the overall excitement of the day which did it – all three taken together, perhaps – but, although my conscience told me that I should be out and about looking for Holmes, my weary body gave up the struggle, and I knew nothing more until I awoke next day to find daylight streaming in at the windows, and Dubuque standing over me, regarding me anxiously.

'You have slept well indeed,' he said.

'Is it late, then?'

'Nine in the morning, no more. How do you feel?'

'A good deal better,' said I, feeling my head. 'Head's still a bit sore, but no sign of concussion, or anything serious.'

'Can you face some breakfast?'

'I believe I could.' I joined Dubuque in the tiny kitchen, and he helped me to coffee and rolls. 'I am delighted that I did not sleep too long,' said I, 'for we may have a long day ahead of us.'

Dubuque shrugged his shoulders. 'I am with you, of course, but ... where do you propose to begin? This Con-stantine is our only clue, and we have not the slightest notion as to where he may live ... indeed, we do not even think that Constantine is his surname.'

'It may be a forename, though. We might start with the police registers, or the electoral roll ...'

'A mammoth task, I assure you!'

'I know, only too well. But I cannot sit here enjoying your generous hospitality, knowing all the while that Holmes ...'

'Calm yourself,' said Dubuque. 'We shall act, I assure you. Only, where to begin?' he added in a troubled voice. He looked at me. 'For one thing, my friend, we must face the fact that Monsieur Holmes may already be ... well, you understand?'

'No,' said I, 'Holmes is not dead ... although the gang must think that I am! Their "chief" made a great point of that, he said he wanted Holmes alive, for the time being.' And I repeated, slowly, 'For the time being, Dubuque!

Yes, he made a great point of that, too! We must act quickly!'

'But I must ask again ... what can we do? Where can we begin?' Dubuque shrugged, then shook himself, as if to aid his thought processes. 'But I am forgetting my manners ... more coffee, perhaps? Another roll?'

'No, thank you. But I would thank you for a match,' and I patted my pockets to find a cigarette. With mixed success: I did not find a cigarette but I did find a solid object – the book I had found in Constantine's house!

'Here!' I cried, taking the thing out and handing it to Dubuque. 'I had quite forgotten this! It may help us ... I found it in a drawer in the room in Constantine's mansion, when Holmes and I were first locked up there. The only thing approaching a clue that I did find.'

Dubuque took the little volume, and opened it at random. 'It is interesting, indeed,' he said, looking at one of the illustrations, 'although one might think it very far from anatomically accurate.' He turned the book on its side, the better to judge, and looked at me. You are a doctor, *mon ami* ... tell me, did ever you see a man ...'

'Not the damned book!' I cried. 'There is a piece of paper in there, to mark the place ...'

'Ah, yes.' Dubuque took the half-sheet of paper out, and regarded it carefully. 'It is curious, too, this ... listen! "Five silk shirts, eleven collars" ...'

'You are looking at the wrong side!' I told him. 'Turn it over ... there is a crest, you see?'

Dubuque turned the paper over, glanced at the top of the page, and shrugged again.

'Well?' I demanded.

'It can have nothing to do with the gang, I assure you,' said Dubuque.

'How can you be so sure of that? It seems to me to be a most important clue!'

'But this crest ... there is no mystery there, my friend! Why, I know it well enough without referring to any textbook. It is the crest of Monsieur Huret!'

'Huret? You know the crest, then?'

'Just so. He is well known, rich ... I assure you that he could not ...'

'And he has an attractive niece,' said I. 'A niece who just happened ... oh, quite by chance! ... to bump into me, and spent an hour or so questioning me, asking was I English, was I a doctor ... oh, Lord! How stupid I have been! Holmes, Holmes, never was your contempt more deserved! Well, I can at least attempt to retrieve the situation now that I have at long last managed to see what has been staring me in the face all along!'

Dubuque had been regarding me with a strange look on his face whilst I reproached myself thus. Now he asked me, 'Do I understand that you have met Monsieur Huret's niece?'

'I did. And, as I say, she spent some considerable time questioning me. And I have no doubt but that she ran straight back to her uncle to tell him the answers. Well,' said I, making to stand up, 'we must go round there at once, of course, and confront this Huret!'

Dubuque laid a restraining hand upon my arm. 'I beg that you will sit down, and listen to me for a moment,' he said very quietly.

Impressed by his calm demeanour, I sat down. 'Well?' I demanded.

'As an Englishman you can scarcely be expected to know this,' said Dubuque seriously, 'but Monsieur Huret is, I assure you, entirely above suspicion.'

'But ...'

'No! No buts! Listen! Monsieur Huret has no title, true, but he is an aristocrat of the old school, nevertheless ... one of the oldest families in France. Well known ... yes! ... I told you that I recognized his crest at a glance, and so would half of Paris, I assure you! Rich ... of course! But there is more to it than all of that. He was a personal friend of the President, you understand? He is not himself a Deputy, but he wields great political influence ... why, rumour has it that the President consulted Huret over the appointment of several ministers. You see now the sort of man he is? You see how silly are your suspicions of him?'

'And for all that,' I said, 'he wrote a note to Constantine!'

Dubuque gave a great shrug of his shoulders. 'And what of that? A man like Huret, he writes a dozen notes each day! Two dozen! Why, the main part of the note itself is missing ... it may have been an invitation, a reply to an invitation ... such a man, he gets requests, you understand, petitions, people asking for help ... it may have been something of that sort!'

'It may not.'

Dubuque looked round – in his own apartment, mark you! – and lowered his voice before he continued. 'What would you do, then?'

'Well, I would go to his house, and ask if he knows this Constantine. With tact and delicacy, of course ... that is understood. But he may be able to help. After all, if he is an honest man, if he has nothing to hide, he would wish to help the police.'

Dubuque shook his head. 'I dare not! And I beg that you yourself will not dream of such a thing! I do not know how matters stand in England, of course; but imagine that my old friend Lestrade had found a clue which implicated ... oh, I do not know ... the Duke of Balmoral, let us say.'

'I am by no means sure that there *is* a Duke of Balmoral, you know,' said I doubtfully.

'*Mon Dieu*! It is an example only, you understand! This clue, it is an important clue in an important case, and it implicates a relative of Queen Victoria ... tell me, Doctor, would Lestrade go at once to Buckingham Palace and knock upon the door, demanding to be let in to interrogate the Duke?'

'H'mm. I take your point. And this Huret, do you really tell me that he is so important?'

'As I have told you. Now, I would wish to do what I can, of course, for Monsieur Holmes ... but one must think of one's career; one's pension. And besides, it is out of the question that Monsieur Huret should be involved in any criminal activity. You may rely upon that.' Dubuque sat back, then said, 'But I am forgetting! We have not yet studied the real clue of this piece of paper!'

'And what may that be, pray?'

'Why, the laundry list!'

'Oh, really, Dubuque! What can ...'

'I beg that you will read it carefully,' he told me, passing the paper back to me.

'Oh, very well, then!' I read aloud, '"Five silk shirts, eleven collars, one pair silk drawers, two pairs silk socks ..." Dubuque, I know you mean well, but what on earth ...'

'It is a curious list, though, is it not?'

'Well, it certainly reveals a love of ostentatious display at the expense of personal hygiene. But ...'

'Read on, if you please.'

'"... sixteen pairs linen sheets, single; six pairs ditto, double; fifteen pairs cotton sheets, single ..." Good Lord!'

'Continue!' said Dubuque, a smile on his face.

'"... nineteen blankets, single; six ditto, double; twenty-six cotton towels, hand, quality; fifteen ditto, ordinary; twenty-four, quality, bath". 'I sat and stared blankly at the thing.

'It is odd, that, is it not?' asked Dubuque with a smile.

'Odd? I should think it is! Dubuque, what on earth can this mean?'

Eleven

Dubuque shrugged his shoulders. 'As to that, I cannot say. But it is very strange.'

'I cannot disagree with you there.'

Dubuque stood up. 'I must leave you now,' said he. 'We are very busy, you understand, since the assassination of the President. We must have extra men whenever a politician appears in public, and so forth.'

'And Holmes?' I asked with some desperation.

'If we had something to go on ...' and Dubuque ended the sentiment with another shrug. 'But I cannot remain here just talking about it, you understand! I would like to help Monsieur Holmes by all means, but we do not even know where he is ... not even a hint, a guess, as to where he may be!'

'If only I could find this Constantine!'

'We have tried.' Dubuque looked for his hat and coat. 'Do you propose to remain here today, to rest perhaps? It might be as well, and I shall return as soon as I can. Why, you might even puzzle out the meaning of the laundry list!'

'I think I may take a walk outside,' said I. 'It looks a glorious day, and I could use some fresh air and gentle exercise.'

'Well, here is a spare key,' said Dubuque, handing it over as he spoke. 'Treat my apartment as if it were your own.' He stared hard at me. 'But you were not perhaps thinking of anything foolish, were you? You did not intend to go to Monsieur Huret's house, for example?'

'Good Lord, no!' said I mendaciously. 'Such a thought never occurred to me!'

'Because I have already told you that it would be most inadvisable to do so. You understand, if you did anything so fantastic, and Monsieur Huret called the police to protest, I could not protect you? There are questions already, as I have said, about this jewel robbery of yesterday ... fortunately you yourself were not seen anywhere in the vicinity! But, if Monsieur Huret makes a complaint ... you comprehend? I would try, *bien entendu*, but the most I could ask would be that you should be allowed to serve your sentence here, in France herself, and not be sent to Devil's Island! So, be careful!' And with that, the honest Dubuque let himself out.

I sat and thought for a time. Despite my own disclaimer, and Dubuque's warning, I fully intended to go to Huret's mansion and ask to see him. That much I had decided. But what then? I could hardly accuse Huret point blank of being a criminal mastermind, of plotting to overthrow the government of France! No, perhaps not that exactly – after all, Dubuque might be right, my suspicions might be unfounded. But on the other hand, I could ask, civilly enough, if Huret knew a Monsieur Constantine, could I not? Well, whether I could or could not, that was what I proposed to do. If this Huret knew every minister and half the Deputies – nay, if his grandfather had been First Consul and his father President! – I should confront the fellow and ask him what the devil he had done with Holmes. I loaded my revolver – I would not be found wanting there again, at any rate! Then I rummaged in a cupboard and found one of Dubuque's hats to replace my own unserviceable headgear, then I set out for the Avenue du Bois de Boulogne.

For all my resolution, when I arrived outside the imposing house where I had encountered Mademoiselle Huret, I stood there hesitant. All the objections which Dubuque had raised – and many which he had not – struck me with their full force. What if I were wrong, after all? The circumstance is not one which has been entirely unknown in the course of my eventful life. What if Mademoiselle Huret had bumped into me quite by chance, what if her questions had been merely the natural consequence of an innocent young girl's impulsiveness? What if the whole business of the note were a monstrous coincidence?

As I stood there hesitating, a *gendarme* strolled past. He slowed as he passed me, and looked me up and down with a rather insolent stare. I might have been offended, but I realized that Dubuque's hat was about the only item of my attire that was halfway respectable, for I had not changed my other clothes. To disarm any natural suspicion the policeman might have had, I asked him, 'Is this the house of Monsieur Huret, if you please?'

'Why, yes,' said he, sounding surprised.

'Thank you.' I made as if to enter the gates, but slowed down and looked back as I reached them. The *gendarme* was still looking suspiciously after me. If he had moved along, I should perhaps have turned back and continued down the road myself, but as it was, with that cold stare at my back, I felt obliged to go up to the huge door and ring the bell.

It was opened by an elderly and very proper butler, who looked at me much as the *gendarme* had done. I half expected to be told that the tradesmen's entrance was round the back, but he merely asked, 'Yes?'

'Is Monsieur Huret at home?'

'I regret he is not.'

'Mademoiselle Huret, then?'

He raised an eyebrow. 'No-one is at home, Monsieur.' The door started to close.

'Monsieur Constantine?'

'I know no-one of that name, I regret.' The door continued its progress towards me.

'One moment, if you please!' I cried. 'I have an important message for Monsieur Huret ... you could not tell me where he might be at the moment?'

'I regret I cannot.' He practically sneered at me, 'Monsieur Huret does not always feel obliged to confide in me, you understand!' The door closed firmly in my face.

I stood on the step for a long moment, wondering whether I ought not to have produced my revolver and demanded admittance. Perhaps so. But it was too late for that now. And, in any case, Huret may have known nothing of Constantine – his butler had denied knowing the name. Disconsolate, at a complete loss as to what to do next, I trudged wearily down the drive and into the street. I might just as well return to Dubuque's apartment and rest, thought I, and looked around for a cab.

A tall man brushed past me, and I mumbled an apology. He half turned, bowed, and then – quite unexpectedly – asked, 'Doctor Watson, is it not?'

I was astounded! I tried to stammer out a denial, but before I could utter more than two words my arms were seized by a couple of men who had evidently come up behind me. A callused hand was clamped over my mouth, and I was lifted bodily into a cab, which set off at a cracking pace.

The tall man – whom I now recognized as the man I had bumped into outside the Huret mansion two days before – searched me, whilst the others held me down. He soon found my revolver, and then ordered the others to release me. I sat up, and looked down the barrel of my own pistol.

'Now, Doctor Watson. I think it is time we had a little talk!'

'It is indeed, Jupin,' said I, as calmly as I could manage, for I had now recovered my wits sufficiently to recognize the aristocratic profile and the waxed moustache as belonging to France's most famous thief. In my own defence I should mention that I had only seen him once or twice, and then but briefly, before then, although I had seen his photograph a couple of times. And he was, besides, almost as great a master of disguise as Holmes himself.

Jupin bowed as well as was possible inside the cab. 'Now the formalities are over, perhaps you would oblige me by telling me what the devil is happening?'

'Damned if I know!' I told him frankly. 'I was hoping you might tell me!'

Jupin looked at me for a long time. 'I think you are telling the truth,' said he at length. 'Very well, we shall pool our knowledge. I have had you followed, of course, ever since you came to France ...'

'What!'

Jupin shrugged. 'The customs examination, you understand? Such a great quantity of tobacco could not fail to attract the attention of my man at the station!'

'Holmes and his infernal smoking! Well, you followed us ... what then?'

'I tell you plainly, Doctor, that I was puzzled. First, I think you are here to track down me, Arsène Jupin! That is only natural ... I am, after all, the most famous thief in all France! But then you went to an anarchist meeting, and the police raided the place. Ah, I thought, Mr Holmes and the good doctor, they have come to Paris to smash the anarchist ring! But then you disappeared. Very well, they have returned to England, I think. But then I stroll to the Bois, with a lady ... and who do I see but Doctor Watson, also with a lady? Ahah, I say ... this is the Doctor Watson I know! But wait! I wonder ... the excellent Doctor Watson, he is known as a man about town, a dandy, one would say, his costume is always of the neatest ... so why then is he dressed like the character in his famous story of "The Pox-doctor's Clerk"?'

'It was *The Stock-broker's Clerk*, in point of fact, Jupin.'

'It is all the same!'

'And I thought my apparel quite smart,' I added.

'I say to myself ... "There is something strange in all this!" I would follow again, but I have business, you comprehend? Now, my business is just this ... I have my eye on a certain jeweller's shop, in the Place Vendôme. My man, who watches the place, tells me that two of the biggest rogues in all Paris are there ... and dressed as *gendarmes*! Ohoh, I tell myself ... this is droll, is it not? I take one of my best men, and he and I, we dress as *gendarmes* too! To see the fun, you comprehend? But then, I see Monsieur Holmes enter the shop, and steal the diamonds!

And the rogues, they pursue! But this is a novelty! Very well, Arsène Jupin also likes his little joke! I arrest Holmes, and I take the diamonds!' And he patted his pocket complacently.

'You villain! You struck Holmes!'

'What of it? Monsieur Holmes; and you, Doctor; and I ... we are not academics, we are not intellectuals ... a little tap on the head, it does us no harm! But still I am puzzled. I change my uniform for more elegant apparel, I hide in a doorway, I follow once again. I see Monsieur Holmes dragged from that unsavoury *bistro*. But where is Doctor Watson? I search, I find you in the alley ... I tell you, *mon ami*, I was anxious! But you too have the thick skull, and I see you are unhurt. You may say I was wrong to leave you there, but I am concerned as to what will happen next. So, I send a note to Monsieur Dubuque, and again I watch and follow! And then you call at the house of Monsieur Huret, one of the richest, most famous men in Paris. By now, my curiosity is too great for me to wait further, so I invite you for a little chat!'

'As to the latest affair,' said I, 'it is simple enough. I was looking for Holmes, and I thought this Huret may know where he is.'

'But Monsieur Holmes is hardly to be found at the house of Monsieur Huret!'

'So Dubuque said.' I looked at Jupin, aware of an odd look on his face. 'Jupin, do you know where Holmes is at this moment?'

'But of course! He is in the Avenue Kléber, kept prisoner at the house of Monsieur Duclos!'

'What!' My head ... not for the first time ... swam. 'Duclos, you say?'

'In the Avenue Kléber. We can go there, if you wish.' And he called an instruction to the cabbie.

'Duclos?' said I again. 'Are you sure, Jupin? Not "Constantine"?'

'Well,' said Jupin with a shrug, 'he is Monsieur Constantine Duclos, after all!'

'Ah! Then we have him! Tell me, Jupin, what do you know of this Constantine Duclos?'

'I know he is a rich man, *mon vieux*! Also, he is one of the greatest villains in all Paris! But he is clever, you comprehend ... he hides his villainy under a cloak of good works. And he is not a very nice man; not a likeable rogue, you understand ... not like Arsène Jupin!'

'Quite so. Would it perhaps surprise you to know that this fellow Duclos is the head ... or the second in command, I should say ... of a gang which plans to take control of France?'

Jupin thought this over. 'No,' he said at last, 'frankly it would not surprise me! He is corrupt, ambitious ... but that is a big plan, a high ambition, even for him! You say he is second in command only, though? Who, then, is the first?'

'I believe it to be none other than this Huret fellow!'

Jupin shook his head, just as Dubuque had done. 'I cannot agree with you there, old friend ... Huret, he is above suspicion! I, Arsène Jupin, I tell you this! I would know, I say, if he were a rogue! What do you English say ... "It takes one to know one", is it not?' He leaned forward and looked directly at me. 'But this other affair ... that is different! I have noticed that there is a gang at work ... more than once they have interfered with my own plans, and that annoys me! But to take over France? That is worse! I am ... they tell me ... a villain! But, Doctor, I am a loyal Frenchman! If this Duclos fellow is planning a *coup* then I, Arsène Jupin, shall join forces with you ... and Monsieur Holmes ... to foil him! Thus, we shall save France ... and remove this other gang, these villains who would spoil the sport of Arsène Jupin! What say you to a truce?'

'Gladly!' I told him, holding out my hand.

Jupin shook my proffered hand, then slapped my revolver into it. 'A token of good faith!' said he. He nodded out of the window. 'You may need your pistol,' he added carelessly, 'for this is the house of Monsieur Duclos!'

We got down from the cab, and I looked at the house with some interest. It was perhaps not so large nor so grand as that of Huret, but it was imposing enough. Under different circumstances, I might have hesitated; but if I had honest doubts as to Huret, I had none at all as to Constantine – or

Duclos, as I now knew him to be – and I set off up the drive, Jupin following. I moved cautiously around the front of the house, and was delighted that I could recognize the side door and coach house as being those I had seen when Holmes and I were here earlier.

'This is the place?' said Jupin, seeing my face.

'I am sure of it! I do not know just what we may find,' I added. 'There may be some danger!'

'Poof! *En avant!*'

I returned to the front door. Taking a firm grip on my revolver with one hand, I rang the bell with the other. After what seemed an age, the door swung open, and I pointed my pistol at none other than my old friend Georges.

'Hello, old chap!' I told him.

'Monsieur! But what ...'

'No time for that, now,' said I, brushing past him and entering the house. 'Is Monsieur Constantine ... or Monsieur Duclos, or whatever he may be calling himself today ... is he at home, then?'

'I regret, Monsieur, he is not. Perhaps you would care to wait, or to leave your card?'

'Wait? I think not, Georges. No time, you understand? As for a card, well, I seem to be quite out of them. No, this ...' and I waved my revolver at him – 'this will have to serve as an introduction. This is Monsieur Jupin, whose reputation may be known to you. He has no card either, but he has his own revolver! Now, is there anyone in the house?'

'No-one, Monsieur! I assure you ...'

'No, Georges, it is I who assure you ... I assure you that we are going through this house together, the three of us ... with you in the lead, in case we should chance upon something unpleasant and unexpected. And I further assure you, my friend, that if I have the least cause to be suspicious of your behaviour, I shall shoot you. And if by some chance I cannot shoot you, why, then Monsieur Jupin will! Is that understood?'

'Why, why, yes, Monsieur,' he stammered.

'I think we might usefully begin with the room in which Holmes ... that is, my friend ... and I spent so many happy hours,' and I urged him towards the stairs.

Georges seemed to entertain grave doubts about the whole enterprise, but with the threat of my revolver and the toe of my boot alike I propelled him upstairs until we stood before the door of the room which Holmes and I had formerly occupied. The key was in the lock on the outside. 'Is the door locked?' I asked.

'I do not know, Monsieur.'

'Stand aside.' I rattled the handle of the door, which was indeed locked. 'Unlock it!' I told Georges.

He did so.

'Now open the door and go in ... but be careful what you do!'

Georges timidly pushed he door open and took a step or two into the room. 'Why ... Monsieur!' he cried, with every indication of astonishment.

I followed him inside, and was horrified to see Holmes's inert figure lying, bound and gagged, upon the bed!

'You villain!' I cried at the unfortunate Georges. 'Untie him at once! By heaven, if anything has happened ...'

'But, Monsieur! I assure you, I know nothing of this! Monsieur Constantine, he gives me the orders, do not unlock ...'

'Untie him, I say! This instant!'

Georges' fingers were trembling too much to be of any use, and so Jupin untied Holmes, who sat up with some difficulty and rubbed his arms where the ropes had bitten in.

'Monsieur Jupin!' This is a pleasure! Delightful to see you, Watson!' said he, with his old liveliness unabated. 'I will be honest ... I had all but given you up for dead!'

'Takes more than a tap on the head to kill me, Holmes! Let's get you out of here ... we cannot say when this rogue Duclos may return with his cohorts ... or his master.'

'Duclos?'

'Constantine Duclos, Holmes. That is his name.' To Georges, I added, 'You, old friend, must spend some time locked in here,

I am afraid, at least until Duclos ... or the police ... can release you. I shall not, however, tie you up.'

'But, Monsieur!'

'That is to say, I shall not tie you up provided that you behave yourself!'

'Monsieur ...'

I ignored him, and Jupin and I helped Holmes out on to the landing, locking the unfortunate Georges in the room. 'He may indeed be innocent,' I told Holmes, 'but it is as well to be sure.'

'But how on earth did you know I was here?' Holmes wanted to know. 'And, for that matter, how did you find the house at all? And you, Jupin, what part have you in all this?'

'All in good time.' I offered him my arm, but he refused, saying that he was well enough.

'Perhaps a glass of Monsieur Duclos's excellent cognac would not come amiss, though,' he added. 'And some food. I have not eaten or drunk anything since last I saw you.'

I took him into the kitchen, and set some bread and cheese before him. Whilst he began work on that, I took a quick look round the rest of the house, but it was empty – not so much as a parlour maid could I find. I took a decanter, three glasses and a cigarette box into the kitchen.

'Ah,' said Holmes. 'A cigarette! Help yourself to brandy,' he added sardonically, as I poured generous measures.

'I shall, Holmes, never fear! Best thing in the world for shock, you know! If you had given me up for dead, I in turn had no idea what those rogues might have done to you. Indeed, it might be as well if we did not linger too long over our brandy, for we cannot say when Duclos might come back.'

'I think we have a few minutes,' said Holmes thoughtfully, 'for I gathered from what I managed to overhear that some great action is in prospect. Would to heaven that I knew what it might be, and where it is to take place!'

'You have no idea at all?'

'They were careful not to say too much, even with me in my helpless state. But you did not tell me how you found me.'

'It was nothing,' said I, with what modesty I could manage. 'Jupin's doing, in fact.'

'Ah.'

'But I have not been idle, Holmes! I found a clue when we were here last, but I did not understand its meaning until just lately. Then there was a girl ...'

'Ahah!'

'She led me to the truth, indirectly, Holmes! It was her name which enabled me to work out the clue, so to speak!'

'Ah. Then everything was for the best, after all.' Holmes looked at Jupin. 'You look sceptical, my friend.'

'Ah, Doctor Watson, he has some strange ideas!'

'Well,' said Holmes, 'I shall insist on the full details later, of course, but the main thing now is to find this mysterious "chief", and then to see if we cannot deduce what he and Duclos have in mind.'

'Oh, I quite forgot! The excitement, you know! I myself am convinced that the "chief" is a man called Huret. I am certain of that, although Dubuque and Jupin have some reservations ...'

'What!'

'Dubuque and Jupin have some ...'

'No! I meant, the name of this head of the gang! Huret, you say?'

'I am certain of it, Holmes.'

'But how on earth ...'

'His crest was on a note ... a bit of paper, I should say ... that I found in the room upstairs. The rest of the note was gone, so I attached no real importance to it.'

Holmes subsided. 'And you have tried Duclos's tailor, then? His wine merchant?' he asked with heavy sarcasm.

'Holmes?'

'A note! Part of a note, rather! It is surely a slender clue, Watson! Part of a note from this man Huret to Duclos! If the note had been there, and if it had been incriminating ... then, of course ...'

'You are right, *mon ami!*' said Jupin, delighted. 'I tell the doctor here, no, you are mistaken. Dubuque, he has said the same thing!'

Holmes looked hard at me.

'Nevertheless, Holmes,' said I, reluctant as always to abandon my own theory, 'this Huret knows Duclos! At the very least, he is what Lestrade would call "an associate of known criminals". If Huret's butler had been more forthcoming, I am confident I should have made more progress! Still, as things turned out, our friend Jupin here found me, and brought me to you.'

'And very glad I am that you are here, my dear fellow!'

'What next, Holmes? It seems to me that we have not got very far after all.'

'Well, at least I am untied, Watson, so I should have said that you did excellently, old friend!'

I mumbled something appropriate in response to this unaccustomed compliment.

'For the rest,' Holmes went on, 'I agree that we appear to have little enough to work with. We know that something is happening, and this very day ... but we do not know what or where. On the credit side, however, we are at liberty ...'

'And armed,' said I, showing him my revolver.

'... and armed, and we have the run of Duclos's house, for I do not think there is anyone here save old Georges.'

'Yes! We must search the place!'

Holmes nodded, and got up. 'We must.'

Search the place we did, but with only mixed success. There was nothing that might be called incriminating, or even mildly suspicious. Even in a room which Duclos evidently used as a study, there was nothing out of the ordinary. However, in the study we did find several letters – all innocuous, invitations and the like – addressed to a 'Monsieur Constantine Duclos'.

Holmes nodded at Jupin. 'He called himself "Monsieur Constantine".'

'And "Constantine" is indeed his first name. Simple, but effective, is it not?'

'Indeed.'

'One thing bothers me, though, Holmes,' said I. 'I can see why there is nothing here that might tie him to the gang, that is clear enough, he wants to keep up the façade of respectability.'

'And he has succeeded ... and would still succeed, Watson. We have found nothing here; Dubuque, were he to search, would find nothing.'

I nodded. 'That is all very well, Holmes. But then why did this ... Duclos, as we now know him to be ... why did he risk giving the whole game away by bringing us, two anarchists, for all he knew, back here?'

'Ah, but then he was flustered, Watson! He had just seen me kill three policemen, you remember! He might, it is true, have taken us to the *bistro*, the regular meeting place, but it was evening, Jean-Paul and the rest would not be there. No, this Monsieur Constantine Duclos decided to hide us here, thinking that we would be gone next day ... as we were ... and that we could never discover his real identity. And he was almost right ... but he had not reckoned with Doctor John H Watson! Or with Monsieur Arsène Jupin!'

Two compliments in one day! I was so staggered that I was obliged to take another glass of brandy. 'We might question Georges,' I said.

'Oh, I think that would be pointless. Georges is a servant of the old school, trained to turn a blind eye to his master's little secrets and indiscretions. You could interrogate him for a week without learning anything of any value.'

'You may be right, Holmes, but it is surely worth ...' and I broke off as there was a loud knocking at the front door. I looked at Holmes. 'Duclos?'

'It may be. Are you ready?'

I nodded, and took out my pistol. We made our way to the door, and Holmes looked a question at Jupin, then at me.

We nodded, and Holmes pulled the door open. There stood Dubuque, with a couple of uniformed *gendarmes*.

Dubuque looked at me, then at Holmes, and finally at Jupin. 'I had expected to find Doctor Watson here,' said he, 'but to find Monsieur Holmes as well ... that is an unexpected pleasure! And ... of all people ... Monsieur Arsène Jupin!'

'Dubuque!' said I. 'How did you find us?'

'I returned to the apartment with my news, but you were not there. I think, where can he be? Monsieur Holmes, Doctor

Watson, they are not the only ones who can reason things out, *n'est-ce pas?* Dubuque, he too can make the deductions. I say to myself, the Doctor has promised not to go to Monsieur Huret's house, he has sworn not to disturb Monsieur Huret, so that is undoubtedly what he plans to do!'

'I don't see …' I began.

Dubuque waved this aside. 'Very well! I go to Monsieur Huret's house. I see the butler … has a man of such-and-such a description been there? Of course, Monsieur, but he has left! I think furiously, *mes amis!* Tell me, I ask the butler, does Monsieur Huret perhaps know another gentleman, a Monsieur Constantine? He looks at me. He frowns. Does Monsieur perhaps mean Monsieur Constantine Duclos? All is clear! I think … Constantine Duclos! Constantine! The mysterious Constantine, at long last! I tell you, my friends, I had my doubts as to this Constantine's very existence, but now I believe everything! I ask the butler … the address? He tells me, and I come here at once.'

'Well,' said Holmes, 'I am delighted to see you. Watson here has told me something of what has happened, although I must confess that I am not absolutely clear as to all the finer details. But I understand that Watson has a suspicion that this man Huret is somehow involved. We must do two things, I think. First, we must set men here to wait for this Constantine Duclos, for we know for a fact that he is involved … these men of yours can do that, Dubuque. And second, the four of us must return to Huret's house at once and confront him, get him to give some account of himself.'

'I regret, Monsieur Holmes, that that will be impossible,' said Dubuque, with some evident embarrassment.

'Oh? And why, pray?'

'Because … I beg you will believe that I regret it most deeply … I must ask you to accompany me to the Palais de Justice. Monsieur Holmes, you are under arrest!'

Twelve

'Under arrest?' said Holmes, looking at Dubuque blankly.
'But of course!'
'And what the devil for? Upon what charge?'
'Why, the jewel theft in the Place Vendôme!' said
Dubuque.
'Oh, that!' Holmes seemed to recover some of his old
equanimity. He smiled at me mischievously. 'I thought
Watson and Jupin would have explained all that to you ...
they seem to have solved everything else between them!'
'Holmes does not have the diamonds!' I told Dubuque.
'But then ... ah!' Dubuque looked at Jupin, and then at the
two *gendarmes*. Jupin seemed to tense himself, for all the
world like a tiger about to spring.
'Jupin,' said I, 'we must work together now! For France!'
Jupin considered this. 'You are right,' he said. He took a
morocco leather case from his jacket, and handed it to
Dubuque with an elaborate bow.
Dubuque opened the case, glanced at the contents, then
bowed to Jupin in his turn before putting the case carefully in
his pocket. 'That at least is something!' said he. 'But still, you
understand ... the examining magistrate ... he must be
informed at once. He must be told what has happened, and
then it is up to him. Now that the diamonds are recovered,
one or two small matters, small discrepancies, so to speak,
may be overlooked.'

'It will all become clear,' said Holmes. 'Of course, it would become clear a good deal quicker if we could but lay our hands on this Duclos, or this other fellow ... Huret, is it?'

'As to that,' said Dubuque indifferently, 'Monsieur Huret is with the Minister of Justice. A private meeting. That was my news, that was why I returned to my apartment to see Doctor Watson. To tell him how silly were all his suspicions of Monsieur Huret!'

'Huret is meeting the Minister of Justice?' asked Holmes.

'Of course! They are having luncheon, and then will talk, one has no doubt, over the brandy and cigars. As I told the Doctor, Monsieur Huret is an important man, a man very close to the government.'

Holmes looked rather ruefully at me. 'One's deductions cannot always be correct, Watson,' said he. 'At least we shall have this Duclos fellow, or Constantine as he called himself.' He looked at Dubuque. 'We shall have him, shall we not?'

'Oh, without a doubt! He has kidnapped you, after all!'

'And the other business ... his involvement with the gang?' asked Holmes.

Dubuque looked embarrassed. 'You have proof?'

'Well, there is the testimony of Watson and myself.'

The look of embarrassment on Dubuque's face deepened considerably. 'The testimony of a man accused of stealing diamonds, you understand!' said he.

'Jupin could confirm my story! The diamonds, as you say, have been recovered!'

'Jupin? No offence, *mon vieux*, but, after all, you had the diamonds in your possession!' said Dubuque. 'And then you have a certain reputation! I myself have faith, but the examining magistrate will ask "Had Dubuque not arrived, who can say what might have happened?" You comprehend?'

Jupin bowed.

'You must appreciate my position,' Dubuque told Holmes.

'Oh, of course! Well, I suppose I shall have to face the examining magistrate, and do what I can to mitigate my own crimes, and those of Monsieur Jupin.' Holmes did his best to say it lightly, and he all but succeeded, but I sensed the defeat in his voice. The only charge we might lay against this Constantine, or Duclos as we now knew him to be, was kidnapping Holmes. And even then a clever man could easily claim that it was not kidnap at all, but legitimate arrest! Holmes was, after all, wanted in connection with the theft of diamonds – diamonds which had been found in the possession of the noted criminal, Arsène Jupin!

If I were Duclos, I told myself, I should not even appear in the matter at all. I should tell the police that I had been out of the house, that Holmes, wanted as a jewel thief, had broken in, and that Georges, the old and faithful retainer, had overpowered him and was just about to call the police when the ruffians Watson, Holmes's partner in crime, and Jupin, the notorious thief, had also forced their way in and released their villainous confederate! That way, Holmes, Jupin and I would get fifteen years apiece on Devil's Island, and Georges would get a medal!

I groaned aloud at the thought. 'If only we had another clue!' said I.

'But we have!' said Dubuque sardonically. 'You are forgetting the famous laundry list!'

'Laundry list?' said Holmes, puzzled.

'Oh, pay no attention, Holmes!' I told him. 'He's trying to be funny.'

Dubuque shrugged, but then his attitude suddenly changed. 'But no!' he cried. 'I was joking, but after all it may indeed be a clue! It may be that Monsieur Holmes can see what we cannot ... I have to do my job, you comprehend, but I have known you a long time, Monsieur Holmes, and would do everything I can to help you.' He turned to me. 'Have you the list?'

I took it from my pocket. 'That was what I found in the room upstairs,' I told Holmes. 'It is an odd list, but I cannot see what it might tell us.'

Holmes studied the list intently. Despite the grim circumstances in which we found ourselves, I almost smiled at his expression.

141

'This could be the clue which solves the whole case, Holmes!' said I, trying to cheer him up.

'Well, it might at that! It is an odd list, I agree, but it is surely not entirely inexplicable?'

'Well,' said Dubuque smiling, 'it is a curious household which has but one pair of drawers to that vast quantity of bed linen and towels, surely?'

'It is not a house,' said Holmes. 'It is an hotel.'

'An hotel?' said Dubuque.

'Yes, of course,' said I, triumphant, 'an hotel! It cannot be anything else, surely? An hotel; and an expensive one; and a small one ... sixteen single rooms, and six doubles, and fifteen for the servants.'

'Well, you may be right,' said Dubuque. 'I see I am outnumbered! An hotel? That would explain the vast quantity of bed linen. But how can you possibly tell the number of rooms?'

Feeling much as I imagine Holmes has so often felt when he has explained things to me, I said, 'From the sheets and towels, of course!'

'But there are nineteen single blankets, not sixteen!' said Jupin.

'Then some of the guests felt the cold!' I told him. 'And the towels do not quite agree, so some guests used two! After all, you would not expect the numbers to agree exactly, one blanket or one towel per guest!'

Holmes laughed aloud. 'Well done, Watson!' said he. 'But then ... there may be some twin rooms!'

'Never thought of that!'

'But all is not lost, for the number of permutations is a very limited one ... there might be eight twins, say, and no singles, but there cannot be more than eight twins. So, we are looking for a small, expensive hotel ... there cannot be so many that the number is unmanageable, even in Paris!'

'I will allow you an hotel, but how do you know it is expensive, then?' said Dubuque.

Holmes nodded to me to explain.

142

'For one thing,' said I, 'Duclos and this fellow Huret would hardly use a doss-house! For another, there are clearly servants' rooms ... that is shown by the cotton, as opposed to linen, sheets; and the inferior quality towels. Then, there may be only a few personal items, but they are all silk. And the fact that there are so few surely indicates high charges for laundry?'

'Or that the guests' own servants are doing the washing, perhaps?' said Dubuque, seeming half convinced.

'Which again would indicate an hotel of the first class! The *petit bourgeoisie* do not take servants along on holidays!' said Holmes. 'Watson is right, as always. I wonder if Duclos happens to have a directory of Paris about the place?'

Dubuque went over to the bookcase, rummaged around, and handed me a thick red volume.

I opened it. 'Hotels ... ah, yes.' I studied the lengthy list ruefully. 'There are lots ... ah, but it is not too bad, after all, for there are not so many luxury ones!'

It was Dubuque's turn to surprise us all. 'Try the St Petersburg,' said he casually.

'Why that?' I wanted to know.

'Just, try it first.'

'Very well. Here we are ... "St Petersburg, near the Place Vendôme" ... the scene of the jewel theft! Quite so!'

Holmes frowned. 'Continue, Watson!'

'"Twenty rooms; eight single, four twin, eight double" ... does that agree with our tally, I wonder?'

Dubuque added up on his fingers. 'Well enough,' said he. 'Continue.'

'"Mostly suites; all with at least a private sitting room; expensive (prospective visitors are advised to enquire as to charges in advance) and frequently booked up for long periods ahead, but with an unrivalled reputation for its standards of service and discretion." This looks promising, Dubuque! But how on earth did you know it was that hotel?'

He shrugged, as if it were nothing, but I could tell he was not displeased. 'A lucky guess ... we were looking for a small, expensive, hotel, and the St Petersburg is known to me as being exactly that. The name, as you may imagine, comes from its formerly being used by the Royal house of Russia ... indeed, I think it was once an hotel in the old sense of the word, a town house in Paris for the Tsar, though I cannot swear as to that. But it is right, that ... "discreet" is the proper word!'

'Indeed?' said Holmes.

Dubuque leaned forward and grew confidential. 'The business of state is not always to be conducted openly, in the Chamber of Deputies,' said he gravely. 'There are private meetings, you understand, delicate negotiations, treaties whose contents cannot be revealed until the time is right. The Hôtel St Petersburg has long been known for such things ... if an ambassador arrives, an envoy on special business, and a confidential meeting must be arranged, a meeting which cannot be held in public at an embassy, or at one of the ministries, the choice is always the St Petersburg. I was there myself last week, in the entourage of one of the ministers ... he was talking privately with a special envoy from ... well, perhaps I had better not say, even to you! But I can tell you that the St Petersburg is famous for its discretion, for providing facilities for diplomatic meetings ... and even for meetings of individual businessmen, who do not wish their business too widely known.'

'And possibly even meetings of a more personal nature yet?' Jupin suggested with a smile.

'One has no doubt! The ministers, the ambassadors, the princes ... they are only men like us, after all, *n'est-ce pas*? The St Petersburg presents ... oh, so discreetly! ... its little account ... which is not so little after all, you comprehend? ... and the client pays for silence, for discretion.'

'But that is precisely the sort of place these men would use!' said I.

'Precisely so!' Dubuque threw up his hands in mock horror. 'But do you not see, my friends, that what seems to you a most important clue, a great discovery, is to me nothing more than confirmation of what I already knew? You say that Monsieur Huret would use the St Petersburg ... I say, of course he does! I know, for example ... I tell you this only in the strictest confidence, of course ... that Monsieur Huret met the President

144

himself at the St Petersburg on more than one occasion, when there were senior appointments to be discussed. You see what sort of a man Monsieur Huret is? The President himself sought his opinion on appointments to the various ministries!' He sank back in his chair, and gazed at me triumphantly.

'And yet Huret wrote a note to this villain, Duclos,' I pointed out calmly.

'Poof! I have already told you that there are a dozen quite innocent explanations as to that!'

'That is quite true,' Holmes put in.

'And then Duclos must have visited this Hôtel St Petersburg, for it was here in Duclos's house that I found this slip of paper,' I went on.

Dubuque frowned. 'That is true. Ah, but then we do not know for certain that this laundry list relates to the St Petersburg!'

'The rooms, though!' said I.

'What of the rooms? There are more hotels in Paris than the St Petersburg, after all! It may be nothing more than coincidence!'

'But ...'

'Indeed,' said Dubuque, 'I am by no means happy with your laundry list, I must say! I have my suspicions! For example, if the laundry list is truly from some hotel ... not necessarily the St Petersburg! ... then how came you to find it, not in that hotel, but here in Duclos's house?'

'Well ...' and I broke off. 'I agree that it is odd,' I said lamely. 'But ... well, suppose, let us say, that Huret wrote the note to Duclos ...'

'Which we know is true.'

'Agreed. Duclos visits this Hôtel St Petersburg ...'

'Perhaps.'

'Perhaps. He tears off the bulk of the note, which he does not wish anyone to see ... possibly he burns it, and he leaves the top half ...'

'And why? Why does he not burn the whole note?'

'Well, perhaps he wanted it to mark his place in his book. That was where I found it. The slip of paper is by the side of his bed, let us say, when the servant comes in. She wants to make her list, sees the paper ... torn and discarded ... and starts to make the list. Duclos returns ...'

'And asks for the paper back?' said Dubuque with some derision.

'Well ... perhaps he did not want Huret's crest to be seen? It would link the two of them!'

'You certainly have the writer's imagination, my friend! Did you ever read that curious history of a flea? Telling how he jumped from a beggar to a king, to the bosom of a beautiful woman, from this one to that one? Your tale is like that, it is picaresque ... the slip of paper is here, it is there ...'

'Well, now it is here!' said I hotly. 'If I cannot say precisely how it came to be in Duclos's house, then at least I can see that it proves two things. First, that Huret wrote to Duclos; and I link that with the undoubted fact that Huret's niece was at pains to find out what she could about me. Second, that Duclos has been at this Hôtel St Petersburg, at which you say Huret is a regular visitor. Can you dispute either of those points, pray?'

Dubuque shrugged. 'I do not need to dispute them, Doctor! No, my old friend, there is far too much coincidence here for my simple tastes! Why, the next thing you will tell me is that Monsieur Huret plans some attempt on the Minister of Justice!'

'And why do you say that?' asked Holmes. 'I understood you to say that this Huret is quite above suspicion?'

'But so he is! No, I meant only that the next thing that the good doctor here will be making a story out of is the fact that the meeting between the Minister and Monsieur Huret is being held at the Hôtel St Petersburg ...'

'What?' cried Holmes, Jupin and I all together.

'But of course! Did I not say? But it is all ... what do you say? ... open and above board. We have a man in the hotel.'

'One man only?' said Holmes.

'It is enough ... the meeting is secret ... the hotel is discreet ...'

'And yet the hotel is one that is used by Duclos,' said Holmes. He leaned forward, and spoke earnestly. 'Do you not see, Dubuque, that even if this Monsieur Huret is not a criminal, there is still a danger? Duclos at any rate is, we know, a criminal ... he may plan to kill both of them, the Minister *and* Huret!'

'That is true!' said Dubuque. 'I had not thought of that!'

'At what hour is this meeting arranged?' asked Holmes, consulting his watch.

'Why, now, more or less. The luncheon is ordered, as I said, and then they will talk.'

'We must get to this Hôtel St Petersburg at once,' said Holmes with decision.

'And what of the other matter? What of the examining magistrate?' Dubuque wanted to know.

'Look here, Dubuque,' said Holmes, 'you and I have known each other for ... what ... ten years? You know that I am no thief, that there is a perfectly simple explanation for this nonsense with the diamonds. But, as I understand it, Watson here has uncovered some connection between Constantine Duclos, whom we know is a villain, and this man Huret. Am I correct?'

'Quite right,' I said. 'And a further connection between Duclos and the Hôtel St Petersburg. And now Dubuque says that Huret is meeting the Minister of Justice at that same hotel!'

Holmes nodded. 'Just so! Does it not seem, Dubuque, that our first task is to visit this hotel to ensure that no mischief is planned, or in progress? If Watson is wrong, and Huret is innocent ... if I am wrong, and nobody is in any danger ... and you shall be the sole judge of that, my friend ... then so be it. I shall immediately submit to being taken before all the magistrates you wish. Jupin will do the same. You know I shall not try to run away, or anything of that sort. What say you?'

Dubuque thought about this. 'You really believe that some crime is planned, then?'

'Well,' said Holmes, 'the whole world knows that the President was assassinated only a week ago! I, for one, would not want the Minister of Justice to meet the same fate! Or this Monsieur Huret, if he is an innocent man! Were it not for the assassination, I would perhaps not be so anxious, I might share your scepticism ... but, as it is ...'

147

'Besides,' cried Jupin, 'it is for France, Monsieur!'

'You are right, of course,' said Dubuque, coming to a decision. 'We shall go to the Hôtel St Petersburg, we shall ensure that the Minister is safe! That, at least, we can do without attracting any opprobrium; after all, that is our job.' He looked at his *gendarmes*. 'One of you stay here, and arrest anyone who may come to the house. The other, come with us.' Somehow or other we all crowded into Dubuque's cab, and set off for the Place Vendôme.

Thirteen

On the way, I gave Holmes an outline – necessarily brief, for the Hôtel St Petersburg was no great distance away, and the driver was taking us along at a brisk pace – of what had happened whilst he was *hors de combat*.

'Why did you not show me the piece of paper when first you found it?' was his first question.

'Well, I thought it was nothing very important at first ... just a laundry list! And then the book it was in ... a bit dubious, Holmes! And then ... well, then I'm afraid I rather forgot about it,' I concluded lamely.

'I see. And then of course there was this Mademoiselle Huret?'

'It all seemed perfectly above board, Holmes! Positively innocent!'

'As my old nurse would have said, it was not on its own there!'

'And as mine would have said, every cloud has a silver lining, Holmes!'

He laughed. 'You may be right, Doctor. Although, by the way, it is most unlikely that the young lady is actually his niece! Well, for all my quibbling, you really did very well. You have found this Huret, whilst I was lying helpless, bound and gagged!'

Basking in this unaccustomed praise, but starting to share some of Dubuque's doubts, I said, 'That is, if Huret is truly the man that we seek!'

149

'And if he is not, if he is guiltless, then he may well be in danger, and we may save his life! You found me, did you not? You tracked down Constantine, after all, found his house! And you seem to have performed the quite considerable feat of turning Monsieur Jupin here away from his evil ways and persuading him to work with us!'

'Yes,' said Dubuque thoughtfully, 'it is a puzzle, that!'

'Monsieur ...' began Jupin, hurt.

Holmes held up a hand and laughed. 'We had agreed to an amnesty! Let us first ...' He broke off as we turned a corner. 'Ah, here we are!'

The Hôtel St Petersburg was tucked away discreetly down a side street. It was somewhat larger than I had expected, but then I recollected that all the rooms were suites, and that there were rooms for meetings, private dining rooms and the like. There was an inconspicuous brass plate beside the door, and a uniformed doorman beside the brass plate. The man stepped forward as Dubuque got down, but then seemed taken aback to see the *gendarme*.

Dubuque held up his police pass. 'Where is the manager?'

'Why ... the office, Monsieur ... behind the reception!' stammered the doorman.

Dubuque led us inside, past the startled receptionist, and knocked in a peremptory fashion upon the manager's door. When the manager appeared, Dubuque showed his credentials, and asked, 'Where is the Minister of Justice? And Monsieur Huret?'

'In a private room, Monsieur!'

'Take us there at once!'

'But, Monsieur!' The manager gestured at the *gendarme*. 'I beg you to be discreet! The hotel ... the patrons ... the reputation ...'

'The devil!' cried Holmes. 'Where is the Minister?'

'This way!' The manager set off almost at a run.

The rest of us were hard on his heels, but I was slightly ahead of the others. We turned a corner, and there, lounging against a door, I saw – who but Duclos! He saw me, too, and turned at once, dashed into the room, and closed the door after him. A *gendarme* who had been standing in the corridor stood to attention as our little group reached him.

'There!' I cried. 'Was that not Duclos? Constantine Duclos?'

'Indeed, Monsieur!' stammered the *gendarme*.

'But he is an aide,' cried the manager, 'a secretary of some sort, to Monsieur Huret! Messieurs, will you not tell me what the matter may be ...'

'They are in there, Holmes!' said I, pointing at the door through which Duclos had just gone. I took out my revolver as I spoke.

'Wait!' It was Dubuque who spoke. He stood with his back to the door, preventing our going any further. To the manager, he said, 'The Minister of Justice is in here?'

'Yes, Monsieur.'

Dubuque looked undecided.

Holmes said, 'Dubuque, the Minister may well be in that room ... but so is one of the biggest villains in Paris!'

'Perhaps two,' I added.

Dubuque straightened his back, and pulled at his waistcoat to tidy it. 'Very well.' He gave me a grim smile. 'My job, my pension ... they are in your hands, Doctor!' and he tapped upon the door and opened it.

'What is this?' There was only one man in the room, and he stood up as we entered. I recognized the sturdy figure and the black beard of the Minister of Justice, whose photograph I had seen in a popular newspaper not ten days before, when the President's assassination was the only news which mattered.

'A thousand pardons, Monsieur.'

'Is that Dubuque? What is wrong?'

'Nothing, I trust, Monsieur.' Dubuque glanced round the room. 'Was Monsieur Huret not with you? It is him we wished to see.'

'His secretary, Duclos, called him away ... some urgent message.'

'They left through this door, I take it?' asked Holmes, darting across the room to a second door.

'They did. And who may you be, Messieurs?' asked the Minister with a frown.

'My name is Sherlock Holmes. Doctor Watson, Monsieur Arsène Jupin.'

'Ah! I have heard of you ...' the Minister frowned. 'But there was a *dossier*, a report ... some trouble at a jeweller's shop? And Monsieur Jupin ... well!'

'We are here to prevent a worse crime than petty theft,' said Holmes grandly. He asked the manager, 'Where does this other door lead?'

'Why, to another room, Monsieur. And from thence to the corridor, along which we have just come.'

'Dubuque, you and your men all know Huret and Constantine ... or Duclos, I suppose I should say ... by sight? Yes? Well, get after them ... they must be arrested without delay.'

'And Monsieur the Minister?' asked Dubuque.

'I shall answer for his safety.'

Dubuque nodded, and hastened away with the *gendarmes* after him.

The Minister looked at Holmes. 'It looks as if my luncheon arrangements may have to be cancelled,' said he ruefully. 'Unless, that is, you would care to join me, and explain something of what is happening? For I confess I am at a complete loss. Doctor? Monsieur Jupin?'

'Thank you,' said Holmes. 'Although I fear I scarcely know more than Your Excellency! Perhaps Watson and Jupin here will be kind enough to explain to both of us!'

'Please sit down,' said the Minister, waving his hand at the table and chairs. There was a tap at the door, and a waiter, his face obscured by a silver tray held on his shoulder, looked in.

'Ah, you may serve the meal at once,' the Minister told him. 'There will, however, be four of us, not two, so you had better bring more plates and so forth.'

The waiter gave a sort of awkward bow, and continued into the room. Holmes looked at him curiously. 'Did you not hear ... Watson! Quick!'

I saw Holmes shove the Minister to one side; I saw the 'waiter' produce a revolver and heard the report as he fired; and then I picked up the nearest object, a water jug, and flung it at the waiter. It knocked the tray from his hand, and brought him to his knees, and before he could get to his feet again Jupin was upon him. He fought like the very devil, but Holmes and I joined the fray, and between us we subdued him, just as Dubuque and his men returned, with the man we had known as 'Constantine' between them.

The Minister, uninjured but very much astonished by what had happened, got to his feet in his turn and brushed his coat down. He took a close look at the waiter.

'Why,' said he, astounded. 'Monsieur Huret? But what ... why ...'

'Why did he shoot at you?' said Holmes. 'Because he plans to take over the government of France. Why is he dressed as a waiter? Now, that is interesting.' He went over to Huret, and looked him up and down. 'We have not had the pleasure of a formal introduction,' said he. 'But I did know that you were a master of disguise. Indeed, I believe that you actually had the nerve to impersonate me, on one notable occasion! On that occasion, although I was able to spoil your plans, I was unable to see you arrested. I must say that I was fooled for a moment by your waiter's costume. And I must compliment you on the quick-witted way in which you decided to assume it.'

He moved on, and looked at 'Constantine' next. 'And you, Monsieur Constantine ... or is it Duclos? We do keep bumping into each other, do we not? But I fear that this will be almost the last time. The next time we see each other it will be across a courtroom ... and then it will indeed be one last *adieu*.'

The *gendarmes* led the two villains away, and the Minister shook his head. 'I am still at a loss as to what has happened,' said he. 'But I evidently owe you my thanks, Monsieur Holmes ... not to speak of my life! And you too, Dubuque ... and Doctor Watson ... and Monsieur Jupin ... but where *is* Monsieur Jupin?' he added, looking round the room.

'Jupin?' Holmes looked round. 'Ah, well,' said he, 'Jupin is evidently a modest, self-effacing fellow who shrinks from too much publicity!'

'Or from too close an association with the Minister of Justice, perhaps?' added the Minister, a twinkle in his eye. 'Perhaps we could find another restaurant, and discuss the matter more fully … for I confess that the St Petersburg is a little too lively for my taste just now!'

'Things should be a little quieter now, though, Your Excellency!' said Holmes.

Dubuque nodded agreement. 'All's well, Monsieur,' said he. 'We even have the diamonds!' and he patted his coat pockets. Then he patted them again, and his face fell.

'The diamonds?' asked Holmes.

'The diamonds!' said Dubuque. 'The devil!'

'Jupin!' said I, and we looked at one another for a long moment. Then Dubuque swore most foully, turned and ran out of the room.

That is almost the end of my tale. Except that, as we left the Hôtel St Petersburg in a bunch, the criminals between us – much to the scandal of the manager and the doorman, I may add – I noticed a carriage across the road. And in the carriage, a young woman, blonde, attractive – Marie! Perhaps I should have spoken; perhaps Holmes's scurrilous surmise had been correct. But I remained silent, and if I chose to believe that she *was* his niece, well, I cannot see that it did any real harm.

Holmes and I had a cab to ourselves on the way to the Palais de Justice, and he leaned across to me. 'I have a good many questions for you,' said he.

'I fear I have but few answers,' I told him, 'for a good deal of it has been over my head! Jupin, and so on …'

'You spotted him, of course?' said Holmes. 'He was standing opposite the hotel when we left.'

'Jupin? Was he, indeed? No, I never saw him! Why did you not say something, Holmes? Dubuque was almost frantic!'

'Oh, I could not begin to tell you. Sentiment, perhaps?'

'No place for sentiment in detection, Holmes!' I told him sternly.

'Of course not, Watson!' And he leaned back, and laughed heartily.

Fourteen

'One thing does still trouble me,' I told Holmes, as I struggled with a recalcitrant collar-stud.

'How to fasten a bow-tie?' said he, with every appearance of solicitude. 'My dear fellow, your tailor is surely ...'

'Flippancy ill becomes you, Holmes! And especially not today, of all days. No, I cannot see just what Huret intended when he went to meet the Minister of Justice. Did he originally mean to kill him, do you think, or just what did he intend?'

Holmes polished his silk top hat carefully on his sleeve. 'He did not originally plan to kill the Minister. I had a long talk with the Minister, and it turned out that he and Huret were discussing how best to restore some stability, that "law and order" with which the popular press makes such great play, to the country following the assassination of the President. Huret was for imposing martial law, a strict curfew, and the like, with severe penalties for any infringements. Huret had also, so the Minister says, provided himself with a list of names of those whom he ... Huret ... accused or suspected of wanting to take over control of the government for their own ends.'

'Ah. Those would be men whom Huret feared, I take it?'

'Just so. Genuine patriots, true democrats, men who would oppose Huret's own attempt to seize power.'

'Clever dog! He hoped that the Minister would ... using the legitimate apparatus of the law ... remove those men who might be obstacles to Huret's schemes! It was cunning, though, Holmes! To try to remove his enemies by legitimate means, rather than use a bullet or knife ... for, after all, who would vote for a known crook?'

'There is an innocence about you, Watson, which is totally refreshing,' murmured Holmes. 'Politics is not a game for the unsullied.'

I laughed. 'I did say a "known" crook! But if Huret could achieve his ends without too much obvious villainy, he would be less likely to be opposed by honest men.'

Holmes nodded. 'True. And then, with martial law and the rest, whoever controlled the army would control France. And we may be certain that the man who controlled the army ... and most of the other elements of public life besides ... would have been Huret.'

'Does it not sound just a touch ... melodramatic, perhaps?'

'Perhaps,' said Holmes with a laugh. 'But would you call the first Napoleon melodramatic? After all, just as our old friend Jean-Paul suggested to us, Huret was only doing what Napoleon ... and others like him ... have already done. History repeats itself, you know.'

'I wonder how Napoleon would have managed had there been a Sherlock Holmes around then?' I mused.

Holmes laughed. 'It is perhaps as well that it was never put to the test,' said he.

'Why did Huret keep you alive, then? It would have been much safer to have killed you at once, when he knew your identity. That is what I should have done, in his place!'

'Ah, it is as well for me that you never turned your talents to crime, Doctor! No, there we can only speculate. I have no doubt that he planned to kill me eventually, but that he wanted my death to be part of some grand scheme ... he might claim that he had caught the jewel thief whom the police had failed to catch, let us say, although he would naturally regret that the thief was not taken alive to stand trial. That would bring him to public attention, make the masses look favourably upon him.'

'And then when he made the attempt on the life of the Minister ... had he succeeded, he would undoubtedly have killed you! And Jupin! And me too, Holmes!'

'Indeed, he would. He was, as you say, cunning. And ruthless. Having realized that his first scheme was useless he very quickly produced a second. He assumed his waiter's garb, and planned to kill the Minister, and then us! He would have said that we ... three wanted criminals ... had killed the Minister, and that he, Huret, that is, had killed us in turn. That would send his stock up considerably, would it not? The assassination by known criminals of the Minister of Justice, hard on the heels of the assassination of the President by an anarchist ... that would show that a strong man was needed to take over the apparatus of government. And there would be Huret, the man of action who had killed the assassins ... though, alas, too late to prevent their killing the poor Minister! Why, that incident might easily have been the final factor which would have led to his being swept to power on a wave of popular acclaim, led to his being declared President, or First Consul, or whatever title he had picked out for himself!'

'A close thing, Holmes!'

'As you say. Will you wear your Afghan medal?'

'Oh, yes.' Holmes was to attend a small ceremony, at which he would be awarded the Legion of Honour for his arrest of Huret; and I was invited to accompany him. 'I do not wear it often,' I added, 'for it seems to me wrong to glorify war overmuch. But, on special occasions ... and this is indeed a special occasion. By the by, I find that I was wrong just now ... there is in fact another small point which puzzles me. Why is it that you accepted the Legion when I know that you have so often refused honours from the British government?'

Holmes was seldom at a loss, but this time he looked almost embarrassed. 'It is a silly thing,' said he at length. 'When I was a boy, there was a portrait of one of my French ancestors hung up at home; and he wore the medal of the Legion. It seemed to me ... well, a young lad's dreams, you know, Watson. And, besides, did not your friend Conan Doyle once say something to the effect that there were so many holders of the Legion that it was almost a distinction *not* to be so invested?'

'If he did, I am sure he spoke in jest,' said I. 'And if by some mischance I am wrong, then surely no honour was ever more deserved than this!'

Holmes seldom showed emotion, but he had to clear his throat before shaking my hand and saying, 'Why, thank you, Watson! Are you ready?'

'All ready.'

He hesitated. 'You are really not obliged to come along, you know.'

'Where should a man belong but by the side of his friend, in the hour of triumph no less than in the moment of danger?' said I sententiously.

'But this is almost our last day in Paris, and I am sure that there must be things you wish to do!'

'Not a bit of it, Holmes!'

'It is such a lovely day,' said Holmes, a touch of desperation in his voice. 'The Bois will be looking at its best just now. There will undoubtedly be attractive young women promenading therein,' he added, by way of an extra inducement.

'It will be equally clement this afternoon. And there will be equally lovely Parisiennes to be encountered.'

'I fear that the ceremony will bore you.'

'I am used to ceremony ... and boredom, too ... my dear fellow, after my time in the army. I am looking forward to it. And in any event,' I added, rubbing it in unmercifully, 'not for all the world would I miss the chance of seeing Mr Sherlock Holmes being kissed vigorously on both cheeks by an enthusiastic Frenchman!'

"With five volumes you could fill that gap on that second shelf."
(Sherlock Holmes, *The Empty House*)

So why not complete your collection of murder mysteries from Baker Street Studios? Available from all good bookshops, or direct from the publisher with free UK postage & packing. To see full details of all our publications, range of audio books, and special offers visit www.crime4u.com where you can also join our mailing list.

IN THE DEAD OF WINTER
MYSTERY OF A HANSOM CAB
SHERLOCK HOLMES AND THE ABBEY SCHOOL MYSTERY
SHERLOCK HOLMES AND THE ADLER PAPERS
SHERLOCK HOLMES AND THE BAKER STREET DOZEN
SHERLOCK HOLMES AND THE CHARLIE CHAPLIN AFFAIR
SHERLOCK HOLMES AND THE CHILFORD RIPPER
SHERLOCK HOLMES AND THE CHINESE JUNK AFFAIR
SHERLOCK HOLMES AND THE CIRCUS OF FEAR
SHERLOCK HOLMES AND THE DISAPPEARING PRINCE
SHERLOCK HOLMES AND THE DISGRACED INSPECTOR
SHERLOCK HOLMES AND THE EGYPTIAN HALL ADVENTURE
SHERLOCK HOLMES AND THE FRIGHTENED GOLFER
SHERLOCK HOLMES AND THE GIANT'S HAND
SHERLOCK HOLMES AND THE GREYFRIARS SCHOOL MYSTERY
SHERLOCK HOLMES AND THE HAMMERFORD WILL
SHERLOCK HOLMES AND THE HILLDROP CRESCENT MYSTERY
SHERLOCK HOLMES AND THE HOLBORN EMPORIUM
SHERLOCK HOLMES AND THE HOUDINI BIRTHRIGHT
SHERLOCK HOLMES AND THE LONG ACRE VAMPIRE
SHERLOCK HOLMES AND THE MAN WHO LOST HIMSELF
SHERLOCK HOLMES AND THE MORPHINE GAMBIT
SHERLOCK HOLMES AND THE SANDRINGHAM HOUSE MYSTERY
SHERLOCK HOLMES AND THE SECRET MISSION
SHERLOCK HOLMES AND THE SECRET SEVEN
SHERLOCK HOLMES AND THE TANDRIDGE HALL MYSTERY
SHERLOCK HOLMES AND THE TELEPHONE MURDER MYSTERY
SHERLOCK HOLMES AND THE THEATRE OF DEATH
SHERLOCK HOLMES AND THE THREE POISONED PAWNS
SHERLOCK HOLMES AND THE TITANIC TRAGEDY
SHERLOCK HOLMES AND THE TOMB OF TERROR
SHERLOCK HOLMES AND THE YULE-TIDE MYSTERY
SHERLOCK HOLMES: A DUEL WITH THE DEVIL
SHERLOCK HOLMES AT THE RAFFLES HOTEL
SHERLOCK HOLMES AT THE VARIETIES
SHERLOCK HOLMES ON THE WESTERN FRONT
SHERLOCK HOLMES: THE GHOST OF BAKER STREET
SPECIAL COMMISSION
THE ADVENTURE OF THE SPANISH DRUMS
THE CASE OF THE MISSING STRADIVARIUS
THE ELEMENTARY CASES OF SHERLOCK HOLMES
THE TORMENT OF SHERLOCK HOLMES
THE TRAVELS OF SHERLOCK HOLMES
WATSON'S LAST CASE

Baker Street Studios Limited, Endeavour House, 170 Woodland Road,
Sawston, Cambridge CB22 3DX
sales@baker-street-studios.com

CPSIA information can be obtained
at www.ICGtesting.com
Printed in the USA
LVHW081036051120
670822LV00030B/307